FRACTURED PAST

FRACTURED PAST

BOOK TWO
THE CRIMSON TIME SERIES

EMILY VANDERBENT

NEW DEGREE PRESS

COPYRIGHT © 2021 EMILY VANDERBENT

FRACTURED PAST

Book Two

ISBN   978-1-63730-680-2   *Paperback*

            978-1-63730-769-4   *Kindle Ebook*

            979-8-88504-037-2   *Ebook*

"We are not makers of history.

We are made by history."

—MARTIN LUTHER KING, JR.

For my family, who have been my anchor in the fiercest storms and lighthouse in the deepest dark.

CONTENTS

NOTE FROM THE
AUTHOR

———

I've always been drawn to stories. The way authors create worlds that seem so real and craft characters as complex and compelling as the flesh and blood people around us is a type of magic all its own. From an early age, I knew I wanted to do the same—to wrap my readers so fully in the worlds I create that, even if only for a moment, they could find rest between the pages of my books. I can't say I had a lightbulb moment when I made this decision. It grew as a natural thing, artfully woven into the fabric of who I am.

My love of history grew in a similar way. I can't remember a time I found the depth and complexity of it anything but interesting. When I take a step back and think about it, it makes sense my love of stories would flow into a love of history. For history, at its core, is one giant story filled with worlds that use to be and people as interesting and complicated as our favorite fictional figures. From kings and queens, to peasants, politicians and everyone in between, history is also a sum of individual stories. Each of these stories feed into the larger narrative of history. Some we have been taught from a young age. Others we have discovered on our own volition. But all have played a significant role in shaping the world as we see it today, every beautiful, horrible, lovely, wretched part of it.

Over my years of studying the past, I have found myself more drawn to these individual stories and untold narratives than the broad-spectrum view of history we are so often taught. History, I believe, is in the heart of these individual stories and to truly understand and appreciate it as a whole, we have to start by understanding and appreciating it in its parts. As I've done my own deep dive into the past, I've come across so many incredible women whose stories have gone untold or been misrepresented. Several I can't shake, and I plan to tell as many of them as I can so their legacies are not forgotten. But the ones that have continually pulled me back have been Mary Stuart and Elizabeth I.

While their story is not a new one, the queens themselves and their intertwining narratives are more intricate than they are so often portrayed in books and film. They were cousins by blood, queens by birth and rivals by the circumstances of the times they lived in. As female rulers during an era where such a thing was less than favorable in public opinion, the ties of blood, position, and expectation that bound them together also set them at odds. From birth to death, they existed in a complicated dance that continued even after Mary Stuart was beheaded in 1587. Like many other stories in our past, a single decision or different set of circumstances could have altered the final outcome in ways we have no way of knowing. There are a lot of interesting "what if" questions when it comes to the two queens and their individual and collective story. The *Crimson Time* series, in part, is my exploration of some of those questions.

The *Crimson Time* series is also a byproduct of my own quest for answers. It has become a vessel for healing, or at least I hope it will be. Like Adelaide and many others, I have had my fair share of trials and unanswered questions. I've had to mourn the loss of what was in the past, what is no longer in the present and what should have been in the future. To be honest, I am still walking that line between past, present and future, trying not to lose myself too much in any which one.

The balancing act is not easy. I have a natural tendency to look back, ask questions and relentlessly pursue answers, but I'm slowly learning some answers are not ours to know. Sometimes the healing isn't in the answers themselves, but in the asking and in the person we become by fighting tooth and nail to remember our past, live in our present and hope for our future. We should ask questions and look to our past, both personally and historically. It has shaped and molded us into the people we are, but getting lost in either the beauty or the pain of the past only robs us of a future beyond our circumstances. At the end of the day, it is up to us to choose how we walk that line.

A healing quality exists in art and the creation of it. Artists paint the feelings they can't express in words, and dancers let their feet carry them through movements for the same reason. As a writer, sometimes your story is the hardest to tell. So when words fail me in the communication of my own story, I tell another's. In the case of the *Crimson Time* series, I share bits and pieces of me and my story in each of my characters, but the main narrative is largely Adelaide's. While we are similar in many ways, I am not her, and she is not me. But the heart of what we share is the everyday fight to put the broken pieces of ourselves and our stories back together again.

I don't know what that looks like for me yet. In all honesty, I don't entirely know what it will look like for Adelaide either. But in learning Adelaide's story, those of various women in the past, the bits and pieces of my own and the many stories I have yet to tell, I hope you find the courage to embrace your individual story. Every beautiful, horrible, lovely, wretched part of it.

PROLOGUE

UT PULVIS PULVIS

———

Stars hung heavily in the sky the next morning. Their brilliant glow pinpricked into the inky sky above was the only light guiding Adelaide as she followed the procession of people out of the castle ruins. Dew clung to her high-tops as they left the cobblestone floor and connected with the damp hillside. She clutched the silk shift she wore in her fists and lifted the hem to avoid tripping on the sheer fabric.

A light breeze off the loch shifted the dense fog over the water and tousled her curls, now a loose waterfall of red down her back. She mimicked the steps of those around her—slow and steady in a temperate cadence that matched the movement of the water nearby. Slivers of moonlight illuminated their pale mourning clothes like forlorn apparitions haunting the hillside. Flickers of light sprang to life near the water's edge as the fire of a single flame spread from candle to candle, crowding out the night around the mass of mourners.

Adelaide clenched her fists to keep them from shaking. She'd never been good at funerals, even before she'd had to bury her parents. That day itself had been a blur, consisting of enough condolences and casseroles to last her a lifetime. Grief was a shadow, a constant presence in her peripherals. Some days it was less noticeable than others, but she could never quite seem to shake it. More than a year later, she still found herself turning to talk to her mother or share a joke with her father, but the air beside her only ever stirred with words unspoken.

At the front of the crowd, two wooden boats sat half-propped on shore. Though they were identical, it wasn't hard to tell which one held Barrow, one of the two Kindred they had lost at initiation. Al Capone's descendant Teo stood beside the boat on the left. His hand moved slowly along the bow, absentmindedly tracing the carvings on the Viking-style canoe. Head bowed, he whispered words lost in the wind and crossed himself. He let his hand drop and turned on his heel. His footsteps cut short as his eyes connected with something in the crowd.

Adelaide followed his gaze to a shock of dirty-blond curls, layered like an Impressionist painting. Colden, Van Gogh's descendant, dragged his eyes from the boats to Teo, not quite meeting the young man's gaze. He nodded his condolences, guilt coloring his demeanor. Though it had been an accident, he stilled played a role in Barrow's death. His cousin Elise put a comforting, yet protective hand on his arm. Adelaide half expected an outburst, but Teo simply stuffed his hands in his pockets, ducked his head against the wind, and blended back into the crowd.

Unsure where to go, Adelaide scanned the others blanketing the hillside. As with the gathering in the coliseum, there seemed to be intentional division to the groupings scattered about, but she wasn't quite sure what it was or where she fit. Since bloodlines seemed like a safe bet for division, Adelaide searched for Xander, her childhood friend and descendent of Elizabeth I. Now that she knew they were family as far as history and the Red Rose Society was concerned, maybe it was time to let it all go and forgive him. She was still angry, but after watching Teo say goodbye to Barrow, she better understood why Xander had cut her out the way he did. Knowing what he did about the Red Rose Society, what she was learning, he couldn't risk a scenario where she was in the boat and he was on the shore.

She spotted him near the front of the crowd. Xander's back, arched with tension, was turned to her as he conversed in a low, clipped voice with Matriarch, the Red Rose Society's leader and his grandmother. Her hair fell in a straight curtain around her shoulders. The flicker of candles cast her silver strands in a sheen of copper.

As Adelaide wove her way through the crowd to the front, her eyes skipped over Xander and connected with the young man several steps behind him. Light from the dancing flame softened Kolt's features, recalling Adelaide to her youth and a time when she and Xander had run wild through the woods in her backyard with another boy whose emerald eyes and dark hair juxtaposed his cousin. The memory was fresh and vivid, like the luster of a baked oil painting. If she closed her eyes, she could almost lose herself in its warmth.

"You remembered."

Adelaide shook the memory away, surprised to see her feet had carried her to Kolt and not Xander. Their voices, the only trait they seemed to share, were similar in resonance, but where Xander's was light and airy, Kolt's was smooth and rich. She thought back to the memory—sunlight filtering through the trees, colored leaves crunching beneath their feet, the smell of snickerdoodles fresh on the air, and something else... colored pages shared in secret. Despite the somber atmosphere, she found herself smiling.

"You were the boy with the comic books when we were young. If I remember correctly, you had quite an extensive collection for a kid."

Kolt grimaced. "I was kind of hoping that was one of those details that slipped through the cracks."

"Not a chance. But how did you know it was me earlier?"

He nodded to her feet. "Your shoes. I was with Xander when he painted them for you. I don't think I've ever seen him as proud of a painting as he was when he finished them."

Adelaide looked down at her shoes, caked with remnants of the streets of Paris. She thought back to when she found the box, carefully wrapped in colored paper on the table in her and Xander's clubhouse. She'd run there, barefoot and in the dark, from the neighbor's house a few days after the fire. In her anger and grief, she'd shoved the box off the table. Its solid thud to the ground was enough to pique her interest and distract her as she tore the paper off in furious strips. When she first put the shoes on, she did so out of spite. But they soon became a shield she wielded like the superhero in Kolt's comics.

She glanced at Xander, suddenly aware of all the possibilities that could have been if her world had not become a series of "what ifs." She cleared her throat and inclined her head toward Xander. "I'm actually on my way up there, but your grandmother doesn't seem to be in the best mood. I could use some backup."

Kolt shook his head and his eyes slowly shifted from Matriarch to Xander. "I better stay here, but you should go."

Adelaide shrugged. "That's okay." She turned to stand beside him and faced the front. "If we're all family over here, I guess it doesn't matter where I stand.

Kolt looked like he wanted to say more, but as he did in the hallway when she'd first arrived, he kept his words to himself. Instead, he cast his gaze to the boats. "You'd think after years of these things I'd be used to them by now, but I'm glad I'm not."

Juniper, the Red Rose Society's Keeper and Adelaide's boss from the diner, crossed the bank in front of the boats, coming to rest between the two. A brazier burned brightly behind her. The silver of her head scarf shone like a halo around her pale curls. Fatigue morphed her features as if she felt the weight of Barrow and Jonas' deaths in a physical way, but as she spoke, authority rang in her voice strong and clear as she paid tribute to the lives lost. When she finished, Xander stepped forward and grabbed a torch from Juniper.

Matriarch moved to do the same, but Juniper stopped her. "Adelaide."

The crowd shifted, splitting a path between her and the front. Heat rushed to her face as the weight of their eyes settled on her shoulders. Xander's face shifted as his eyes skipped over her to Kolt a few steps behind her. She felt a gentle push between her shoulder blades, coaxing her forward. She looked back at Kolt as he nodded his encouragement and let her feet carry her toward Juniper. The woman set a gentle hand on Adelaide's arm and handed her the other torch. "This is your part to play now, sugar. The Stuart blood in your veins is more than just a marking of your heritage. It's a birthright."

Adelaide looked to Matriarch, her face a series of hard angles in the night. She straightened her posture and stepped back making room for Adelaide on the side of the brazier opposite Xander. She met his eyes across the flames as he dipped his torch in fire and stepped before the bow of Jonas' boat. She did the same, waves of heat rolling over her skin as she waited for the fire to catch and mirrored Xander, stepping before Barrow's boat. Several men, including both of her friends' fathers, pushed Jonas' boat off shore. Xander watched it glide into the water. He tossed the torch into the heart of the boat, whispering words as the flame ignited. *"Ut pulvis pulvis."* *Dust to dust.*

The men moved on to Barrow's boat, sending it into the water beside Jonas. Adelaide drew her arm back, thinking of Barrow, of Jonas and Brynn, the woman in the alley and her parents as she let the torch go. Sparks caught the dry wood, engulfing the boat and Barrow inside. Wind whipped Adelaide's curls. The boats grew smaller as the seconds stretched before her like the parallel trails rippling across the loch. Fog clouded the boats, the fire still burning brightly in the darkness over the water.

"*Ut pulvis pulvis.*"

1

PERSISTENCE OF MEMORY

———

Adelaide gripped her cardigan tightly as she walked the dark corridor of the castle. Cold, caught between the walls like bated breath, seeped through the cracks of the stone. As it did the first night of her return from Revolutionary France, sleep evaded her. Blood and the stench of Paris' streets had joined the cacophony of smoke and flame ever present in her dreams. She found an odd comfort in the walls. With each late night spent wandering those of the Red Rose Society, they grew steadily familiar beneath her fingertips as she trailed them in the air near their cool surface; close enough to feel the chill, far enough to keep the images at bay. They whispered to her in a way she didn't quite understand, speaking not in words but in flickers of the past there and gone like a faded memory.

Footsteps echoed at the threshold of the corridor. Adelaide jerked her hand back from the wall and stilled. She wasn't necessarily worried about being caught. It wasn't as if she was doing anything wrong or forbidden from wandering around at night, but she didn't want to answer the questions that would come with being discovered out of bed at this late hour. Sidestepping off the main corridor, she concealed herself on the other side of a suit of armor and stood quietly, waiting for the footsteps to pass.

The sound stopped for the span of a heartbeat before beginning again, growing louder as they drew near. Two figures, their pace hurried, rounded the corner ahead of her. Though she couldn't distinguish the figures in the dark, the hushed tones of a man's voice funneled to her through the halls. "... need I remind you what happened last time—"

His words broke off, cut short as the figure in front gripped the man's arm and yanked him into a nearby alcove. "I need no reminder of the past. I see it every day in the face of my grandson and feel it every moment in the absence of my daughter." Rays of moonlight filtered through the small, metal-worked window and fell on a curtain of silver hair. Dust danced in the light like snowflakes in a winter storm as Matriarch, her grip still tight on the man's arm, leaned in.

The man wrenched his arm from her grip. "Tread lightly, Maggie, lest you forget your place and wander too far down a path you cannot turn back from. I mention it only as a reminder of what was almost possible then and might still be possible now should Adelaide's little stunt at the Gala be more than just a fluke. That earring she brought back from France is still whole and shows no telltale signs that it's going to crumble like the rest."

Adelaide gasped, the sound too loud in the quiet of the hall. Matriarch's head shot up, her eyes flying around the corridor. Adelaide's hands flew to her mouth as she shrank back against the antique tapestry behind her. Solid stone met her back before giving way to air and sending her tumbling through to the other side of the wall. Adelaide groaned, rubbing her back. She pulled herself from the floor, the hidden door sliding silently back in place as she rushed toward it. Déjà vu threatened to overtake her as she ran her hands around the wall searching for a way out. Sweat beaded on her palm, still healing from when she had cut it on the broken pendant in sixteenth-century Paris, both a few days and several centuries ago.

Her efforts proving useless, Adelaide kicked the wall. It might have been her saving grace had Matriarch learned she and the man were not alone in the corridor, but the few feet of impenetrable stone might as well be a thousand miles because Adelaide could no longer hear their words on the other side. They had been talking about her, that much she could gather, but who was the man and what had he meant by "last time"? She knew Matriarch's daughter, Xander's mother, had died along with her own parents in the fire, but what did her death have to do with Adelaide's ability to bring the earring back? While it was a question she had no answer to, she was certain of one thing. The Red Rose Society knew something was different about her, and they wanted to know why.

Join the club, Adelaide thought. She wanted to know too, but until she learned more about the Red Rose Society, answers were something she would have to seek alone. While she had forgiven Charlie and Xander for the lies and half-truths told to keep her safe and keep her away, trust was in short supply. She didn't understand enough yet to risk placing it in the wrong hands.

Adelaide ventured deeper into the room, weaving her way between towers of discarded objects. The occasional glimpse of gilded carvings on the walls and faded frescoes overhead spoke of a once-opulent space, perhaps a guest room or a studio. But whatever the room used to be, it was now a shadow of its former glory. She doubted anyone had been there for a while. Cobwebs graced the corners like lace and a thick layer of dust coated every visible surface. Brittle books lay atop a broken sewing table, half concealed by a moth-eaten wedding gown. The bottom half of a marble statue, its name plate too tarnished to read, stuck out from beneath an upturned wardrobe, spilling rainbows of thread across the floor.

The history of these objects ran deep. Adelaide could feel it in the dull ache building behind her eyes—a sensation she had come to associate with her *traces,* as she had coined them. The flashes of history no one else but her seemed able to see. Her headaches had gotten worse since arriving back at the Red Rose Society, but she hadn't had a *trace* as vivid or long as the ones in Paris, just indistinct images floating past her vision like clouds.

Adelaide had done her best to avoid an episode in front of the others, biting her tongue against the pain and keeping her skin from brushing against anything that might have a story to tell. The last thing she needed was for Matriarch or anyone else to figure out there was more to the Adelaide enigma than her ability to bring the earring back intact. Out of everyone, Teo alone seemed to suspect something was up. He had, after all, been witness to a few of her *traces* in the past. Well, he and Barrow, but Adelaide knew the girl wasn't in a position to do much of anything, much less divulge her secret.

Silence hung over the room, save for the shards of silver glass from a broken mirror that crunched beneath her feet. Along with the silence came the absence of eyes that always seemed to follow her like a shadow around the halls, even in the dark. Sure that in this moment she was alone, Adelaide dared to pull her sleeve up, exposing her pale skin beneath. If the Red Rose Society was asking questions about her, she thought it best to figure out the answers before they did.

She reached a hand toward the nearest object, an old oak door propped on its side, and let it hover in the air before grazing the surface. Trailing her finger in the dust along the edge to the knob, she tried to coax a story from the brass. Adelaide could feel it there, dancing under the metal, magnetized by her fingertips, but whatever memories it held remained as immovable as a sword in stone.

Pressure built in her head as her hands moved around the pile, grazing a pipe and a hairbrush, a lock and a quiver in an attempt to relieve it, but each object she touched seemed even less willing to divulge its secrets than the last. Eventually, the pressure subsided to a dull ache, replaced instead by a wave of exhaustion that seeped into her bones. She forced her feet forward in search of an exit, lured by the promise of sleep and a soft light emitting from the back corner of the room. What Adelaide had originally thought was a window letting in the early morning light turned out to be a small door. It sat flush to the wall around a bend in the makeshift path. Intricate molding around the frame appeared long decayed and crumbling away. Light spilled from the crack beneath, the familiar smell of turpentine on its heels.

Adelaide eased the door open. An extension of the adjoining room, the one inside looked pretty much the same as its larger counterpart. Sculptures huddled in the corner like gossiping teens. Paintings of landscapes and large stoic portraits in gilded frames crawled up the walls. The remaining ones stood propped against one another on the floor.

The only difference was the young man inside. He sat on a wooden stool. His back arched beneath his navy t-shirt in concentration. Painter's palette in one hand, the other smoothed fresh paint on the canvas before him. Adelaide watched Xander as he worked, first on the light foam atop the crest of a wave and next on a series of grey-blue smudges like birds above the dark tower of a lighthouse. Memories of her own, spurred by sight instead of touch, seemed to float on the surface of the jeweled waves—a star-studded sky, a warm wind off the coast, words whispered in the dark.

"Looks just like it did in Boston Harbor when we visited a few summers ago." Adelaide wasn't sure what had compelled her to speak, to shatter the fragile familiarity of the moment instead of simply allowing herself to linger in it.

Xander startled, blinking back the fog that settled over every artist's eyes when they were deep in the magic of their craft. His eyes finally focused on her, his features softening. He didn't ask her how she had ended up there but instead dipped his chin, a dissatisfied slant to his lips as he returned to the painting. "Something about the waves isn't quite right, and the golden cast to the sky should be more of a soft champagne than a buttermilk, but I guess that's the downfall of giving substance to memory. It's never quite as beautiful as you remember."

As far as Adelaide could tell, the painting—like Xander's other works of art—was lovely. The moment was worthy of being rendered in paint, and the result a rival to any masterpiece in a museum. She saw none of the flaws Xander could so easily spot, but then again, he was the artist and she was not.

On that same trip to Boston, the two of them had spent hours wandering the city, stopping at the studios of local artists and traversing the halls of museums. They ended the day at the Isabella Stewart Gardner Museum. Of all the masterpieces around the halls, they had spent the most time in front of the Degas. It wasn't the most spectacular of works featured. It wasn't even a full painting like the ones she had seen by him in other museums, just a rough figure drawing of a ballerina that looked as if it had been ripped right from the artist's sketch pad. Adelaide had loved it for its vulnerability, for the way Degas was able to just create in the rawest form without the expectation that others would see it.

Xander, on the other hand, had loved it for the way it showed Degas' progress in his craft, in the increased display of movement and use of lines between it and his final paintings. In that moment, Adelaide wondered if Xander was ever able to appreciate something as it was, instead of for what it could be.

"Sorry," Xander said, mistaking the reason for her silence. "Late night painting always brings out the philosopher in me." He gripped the back of his neck, a slight flush tinging his cheeks.

Adelaide smirked, a nostalgic smile lifting her lips. Avoiding Xander's gaze, she pretended not to hear his words as she flipped through a stack of paintings. She was only half paying attention to the images before her, focused more on his words than the portraits passing between her sleeve-covered fingers. She knew all too well that the right muse brought out the poet in him too. The veil between paint and poetry blurs in moonlight, convincing an artist he can paint words like stars on the canvas of the sky. "Some would say the artist and philosopher is one and the same. So tell me, what human truths are you trying to convey, Aristotle?"

Adelaide had reached the last painting, a half-torn canvas of a woman, when Xander responded. "You're asking the wrong question." Flames from a small fireplace danced shadows across his face, lightening his hair to a pale gold.

She let the frames fall silently back against the wall "What's the right one?"

Xander stood, moving his stool to the side to free a space on the drop cloth. "What do you see?"

Adelaide, resisting the urge to trail her fingers along its still-wet surface, stood before the painting and took in the scene. She knew what she saw when she looked at it: a past she could never return to, a moment she could never get back, a question she was afraid to answer, even now. The girl she was then felt a million miles away from the one she was now. If she was honest with herself, she wasn't sure who that was anymore. With the weight of his silent eyes on her, she wondered what Xander saw when he looked at his creation. What stories, hopes and dreams he could only tell the world in color, and she might only ever know if she coaxed them from the pigment.

She looked over her shoulder at Xander. He remained still, but the tension in his body told her he truly cared to know her answer. As much as she hated to leave Xander with questions unanswered, she couldn't yet tell him the truths of what she saw. As much for her sake as his own. Adelaide knew the moment the words left her lips the painting would no longer be his. Instead of pouring himself into the piece and painting what he needed to, Xander would cast his own story aside and paint hers instead. A brush stroke here and color choice there could be the very difference between him telling the world what he needed to or what he thought it wanted to hear.

"Tell you what, I'll tell you what I see when you're finished."

"Okay." He nodded, the flecks of gold in his dark eyes flashing like stars. "But I'm holding you to it."

Adelaide shivered at the intensity of his gaze as she recalled the night on their trip that they slipped into the crisp ocean while Charlie was sleeping.

"Are you cold?" Xander frowned and picked up a bundle of cloth on the floor near the painting. "Here, I went looking for something to keep me warm one night and found this in the other room." He tossed her the cloth.

She caught it, registering that it was an antique riding cloak only when her skin brushed the tarnished buckle sewn on the front. Images flickered in her mind. She tried to hold them in front of her, splay them out like a deck of cards, but they slipped away faster than they came, leaving her with nothing but the imprint of hooves pounding along a dirt road, green rolling hills and crimson curls streaming in the wind.

"Ad?" Xander asked, his voice muffled as if he were speaking under water.

"Huh?" she said, her own voice sounding distant to her ears.

He waved a hand in front of her face. "You spaced out on me there."

She shook her head and let the images fade as she ran a hand through her curls. "This cloak. Do you know anything about it?"

He quirked his head, taken aback by her abrupt question. "Uh, no. Nothing other than it's Scottish. Actually, you should take it with you. Who knows, maybe it belonged to Mary Stuart."

2

TRACES

———

MAY, 1568
SCOTLAND

When Mary was younger, she used to sneak into the castle stables at night, coax her favorite thoroughbred from its stall and ride until the first hints of dawn light threaded the sky in gold. She relished in the freedom of those secret rides, a speed without hurry, a journey without destination. She gripped her riding cloak tightly and tried to remember that feeling now, but the chill of wind whipping her cheeks and the trill of her heart in her chest refused to let her linger long in the past. Wish as she might, tonight was not one of those rides.

Gunpowder and smoke clouded the landscape, thickened by an evening mist across the Scottish hillside. She welcomed the rain as it cooled her heated skin and ran down her cheeks like the tears she refused to shed. Her crimson curls streamed behind her, loose and free in the spring night. With every hoof beat of the horse galloping beneath her, gunshots echoed in the hills, edging closer. She dug her heels hard into the stallion's flank, but its pace remained consistent, already running as fast as it could on her behalf. Only twenty miles remained in their journey, but she knew this creature wouldn't be able to get her the rest of the way to Dumbarton.

Mary edged the beast around a sharp bend in the road and shifted her weight to keep from sliding in the leather saddle. Her mother, God rest her soul, would roll in her grave if she saw the way Mary was riding, but there were times to be a lady and now was not one of them. Limbs from the trees along the roadside tore at her riding cloak as if James, her half-brother, had employed them to stop her. Many of Scotland's clans might be swayed on James' behalf. Scandal and bloodshed didn't taint his name as it did hers, but whether the rumors were fact or crafted from pure fiction, it no longer mattered. As far as many were concerned, being a woman was enough to convince them of their truth. It didn't help they had John Knox fanning the flames of their hate. Perhaps her greatest sin of all was being born a woman in a world made for men.

The lights of Glasgow burned behind her as she skirted the well-worn paths around the city, careful to keep a wide berth between her and James and his gaining army at her back. The child in her womb shifted, in tune with her emotions but ignorant of the cause. Each night, on bare earth and worn floorboards, threadbare carpet and plush grass, she would cross herself and pray the child she now carried would have a fairer life than its brother, born only years earlier. That bitter-sweet moment, when Mary first held him, small and pink in her arms, felt like a lifetime ago. It belonged to a different girl, a different queen. She wished she could have held time still in that beautiful moment. Before the scandal of her late husband

Darnley's death. Before religion divided her beloved country. Before the Protestants made her son their heir to depose her and James his regent to mock her.

Flawed as the present was, it was hers all the same. Mary knew she had made her choices—black, white and grey as they were. She also knew she would have to live with the consequences of her quick tongue and wayward heart. She couldn't change things any more than she could change the blood coursing through her veins. Blood that said she was Mary Stuart, queen of Scotland, heir of England, and if James, the clans, Knox or Elizabeth wanted to change that, they were just going to have to kill her.

3

TIMEWALKER

Three days was apparently the amount of time it took to recover from a near-death experience hundreds of years in the past. At least that was the amount of time the Red Rose Society had given Adelaide and the others to adjust to their new reality. Before Adelaide even had the chance to process what she'd been through, her best friend Charlie had shown up at the room Adelaide and Elise, Lewis Carroll's descendant, now shared with a color-coded itinerary for their next few weeks as fledgling society members.

As today began day one on the schedule, Adelaide now found herself dressed and awake in the unnatural hours of the morning. Her mother had been a morning person. She was always up with the sun, scribbling in notebooks on the back porch and living half a day before many others finally found the strength to pull themselves from the warmth of their covers. Adelaide, on the other hand, held firmly to the belief that life shouldn't start any sooner than eight o'clock in the morning. Sometimes, even that was pushing it.

She braced herself as she opened the double doors, devoid of the guards that had flanked them the night of the gala. Without the embellishment of decorations and people milling about, the coliseum felt colder than it had before. Her eyes gravitated to the magnificent dome, its jeweled tones of painted scenes the only color in the vast, monochromatic space. She hadn't had much time at the gala to gaze at the frescoes overhead, but they looked different than she remembered. While Xander was the artist, Adelaide knew enough to notice the colors appeared darker and the scenes more crowded together. Had someone repainted them in the time since the gala?

The first time Adelaide had entered the coliseum, she had done so alone with only her questions for company. This time, Elise walked beside her. The smack of the girl's thick leather boots against the marble echoed like the clang of gladiator swords. The white glow of the lights washed her already pale face of color. As they moved to join the small group huddled near the far sidewall, Adelaide couldn't keep her eyes from falling on the floor where Jonas' body had lain. She wondered what would happen if she grazed her hand across the spot. Would it carry vivid memories of Jonas' life or frozen images of his death? She resisted the urge to find out, which wasn't hard considering no one else in the room knew of her ability. No one, that was, except Teo. But even he didn't quite understand the extent of her secret.

She searched for him among the faces, but his was not yet gathered with the Kindred. Come to think of it, Adelaide hadn't seen much of him in the days since their arrival back to the present. The occasional glimpse at the end of a hall or on the opposite side of a room was the gist of their interaction at present. It seemed that every time she entered a room, he was on his way out or vice versa. She couldn't help but wonder if he was purposely avoiding her or if it was just a coincidence. Adelaide had never been one to believe in coincidences, but either way, she wasn't quite sure why she cared. Sure, they had survived something few other people knew about, let alone understood, but that didn't make her and Teo, or her and anyone else in the room, for that matter, friends. They might not be her competition anymore, but that still didn't mean Adelaide trusted them.

They stopped beside Colden, his dirty-blond curls properly moussed despite the early hour. He gave Adelaide a wink and smiled at Elise before returning his gaze to the sheet of paper he held in his hand. His free hand fiddled with the knot of his tie. The navy silk brought out the blue in his chimerical eyes, turning them as deep and dark as a bottomless ocean. "Man, Anson. That friend of yours sure knows how to draft a schedule. Think I could pay her to organize my auctions for the year?"

Adelaide laughed. "Knowing Charlie, she'd probably do it for free." If there was one thing the girl prided herself on, aside from her hacking skills, it was her ability to synthesize even the most chaotic of days into a series of digestible tasks and color-coded activities.

A throat cleared at the front, drawing their attention to Matriarch and Charlie, looking as eager as a sorority girl during rush week beside her. Matriarch clasped her hands in front of her, the grey of her current pantsuit a few shades darker than the silver of her hair pinned at the base of her neck. It was odd to see her at ground level with them instead of up on the dais. But Adelaide had to admit it would probably be even stranger for her to use the platform to address just the five of them.

Skipping the pleasantries, she jumped straight to business. "The Red Rose Society is an organization with roots in sixteenth-century Europe. Founded by my ancestor, Queen Elizabeth I, it continues to operate under the same guiding principles it did at its conception: preserve the past, protect the present, forge the future. You all are now privy to the honor of upholding these three principles as new members of the Red Rose Society. You—"

The doors at the end of the amphitheater opened with a thud as Teo sauntered in. He wore a crisp black button-up tucked into black pants as neatly pressed as his shirt. The suspenders connecting the two bit tightly into the muscles of his shoulders like rubber bands about to break.

Matriarch steeled her gaze at him. "Mr. Capone, might I remind you that I had my choice of several of your relatives to fill the one spot you now occupy. If you wish to keep it, I suggest you work on your punctuality, lest I decide one of your brothers or cousins is more suited for the job."

Teo threw his hand up in a half-wave and closed the last few paces between him and the other Kindred. "I'm here, aren't I?" Not meeting her gaze, he stopped beside Adelaide. She watched him out of the corner of her eye as he rubbed his knuckles. Bruises, ranging from deep purple to yellow, tainted the skin at the base of his fingers. Catching her watching, Teo shoved his fists in his pockets as Matriarch continued.

"As I was saying, a handful of scouts were sent out after you to track your progress and skillsets during your time in Revolutionary France. Based on their assessment, we have assigned each of you a position within our ranks that will best leverage what you have to offer—"

Once again, the doors at the back of the room flew open, this time to reveal Juniper. She walked with a steady but determined pace right past Adelaide to Matriarch's side. The end of her emerald headscarf fell sidelong across her shoulder as she leaned to whisper into Matriarch's ear. Whatever the news was, Matriarch did little to reveal its nature. Her mask of emotion was as steady as a seasoned sailor at the helm. Without a word, she nodded to Juniper and exited the room.

"I wonder what that was about." Elise had voiced it, but Adelaide found herself wondering the same thing.

Juniper cast her gaze over them as the door settled back into place. "Well, I'm not sure how far along Matriarch got into things, but to sum it all up, you each have been assigned a position within the Red Rose Society based on various factors taken from your time in the French Revolution. You will be compensated for your work here, and once your year of training in Scotland is up, you will be stationed in suitable roles around the world. Society members have gone on to work in museums, universities and high-level government agencies. As I call your name and explain your new role, please come forward and grab your packet from Charlotte, who, should you have any questions, will be here to address those for you as they arise."

Charlie smiled, and her champagne curls caught the light as she bobbed on the balls of her feet with the manila envelopes clutched between her arms. She pulled the top two from her grip and handed them to Juniper, who read the names scrawled on the side in Charlie's looping cursive.

"Asena and Sam, the two of you will be in the technology department. Charlotte can show you the way and the ropes when we are done here. Colden, you are the new liaison for Northern Europe. Matriarch will have further instructions for you in her office. Elise, my dear, you will be training with me as a Keeper. And Adelaide and Teo, you are Timewalkers."

Teo's spine stiffened as he took his envelope. Adelaide reached for her own, wondering what, exactly, she had gotten herself into. "What does that mean?"

Juniper, her gaze unwavering, met Adelaide's eyes. "It means your excursion to the French Revolution was not your last trip in time. It was your first.

4

HARGROVE

———

A few wrong turns and a long, silent elevator ride later, Adelaide and Teo finally made it to the basement. The steel doors of the lift opened to a single catwalk strung above a large pit carved from the earth. She was already a few steps down the grating when she realized she was the only one moving. Adelaide looked over her shoulder at Teo. He stood only half out of the elevator, his eyes trained over the side of the railing. As if he could feel the weight of her eyes, he quickly pulled his own from the pit and brushed past her on the catwalk. His arm grazed against hers. The touch was there and gone like a morning frost, but the sensation of it lingered on her skin as she turned on her heel and followed after him.

Thick cables, heavy with the metallic twang of electricity, buzzed overhead. Computers and other electronics whirred and beeped as multicolored lights blinked signals Adelaide couldn't decipher. The main catwalk dead-ended at a set of stairs that descended into the pit. On either side of the stairs, the path continued, splitting off like the parallel arms of a goal-post.

A man in a white lab coat sat in an office chair near the first bend in the walkway. He squinted at a series of screens as identical sets of data scrolled across their surfaces. With his back to them, he was oblivious to their presence as his fingers flew across the keyboard. From what Adelaide could tell, it looked like some sort of binary code, the repeated zeroes and ones signaling messages from one computer to the other in their own language.

Teo cleared his throat, startling the man. He blinked at them through thick, wire-rimmed glasses as he attempted to focus his eyes on their faces. "Who are you?"

"I'm Adelaide. This is Teo. We're your new—," she paused, trying to recall the word Juniper had used, "Timewalkers."

The man glanced at his watch. "Goodness, is it that time already?"

He pushed back from the monitor and stood, proceeding to stroll toward the stairs as if he were on a walk in Central Park. "My name is Dr. Jameson. I'm the lead technologist and analyst for the Red Rose Society."

Adelaide, trying to force her naturally long strides to meet his rather short ones, slowed her pace. Dr. Jameson continued to speak as if reciting a soliloquy while his words tripped over each other faster than his pace, but Adelaide had a hard time concentrating on them. She leaned toward Teo and whispered, "Is he barefoot?"

Teo bristled but let an easy smirk etch his face to cover it. "Sure looks like it."

As they descended the stairs, Adelaide let her eyes wander. The bottom of the pit mirrored the layout of the top, but with even more computers and gadgets scattered around the vast space. Hallways tunneled out in various directions and wound through the bedrock like holes in an ant colony. Several Red Rose Society members hunched over computer stations or stood at buttoned panels reminiscent of switchboards. Cables crawled down the walls to a massive object in the center of the pit. It was round and metallic with even thicker cables radiating from it on either side like the legs of a spider.

Though the three of them had come to rest in the shadow of the object, the man continued to speak, gesturing with his words. "—and that's when I said to the man, the sheer wingspan of a pterodactyl alone would prevent us from being able to bring one back from the prehistoric era. Plus, I doubt we could find anyone willing to share such close quarters with one on the jump!"

He looked at them expectantly in the silence that followed. Adelaide felt bad for having tuned out the beginning of his story and fished for something to say to prove she had been listening. The best she could come up with on the spot was, "What a wonderful story."

He shook his head, disappointment alight on his features. "My dear, if you thought that was a wonderful story, you completely missed the point. I thought you were supposed to be the smart one."

Teo chuckled.

Adelaide resisted the urge to elbow him in the ribs and turned back to the man. "I'm sorry?" Though she also intended it as a sort of apology, it was more meant to be a question.

Dr. Jameson picked up a file from the desk beside him and flipped through the pages. "Let's see. Adelaide Anson, descendant of Mary Stuart. Has shown she possesses a great depth of historical knowledge and the ability to think quickly on her feet, but her sharp tongue and compulsive instincts may prove detrimental to her own safety, that of others, and the integrity of time."

Adelaide scoffed. Her? Impulsive? But then again, she did jet off to Scotland at the whim of a letter. Then she agreed to owe Teo a favor without any real thought about the consequences. Add to it breaking into the Conciergerie, the main prison during the French Revolution, and getting herself blown up by a noxious substance Barrow concocted. Maybe whoever had written that statement wasn't so far off from the truth.

"As for you," Dr. Jameson continued, rifling through Teo's file. "While he puts on an impressive display of hand-to-hand combat, Teo Capone's real asset is not the man himself but the wide array of connections he has. These may prove useful in the continued relations between the Red Rose Society and the mob."

Teo was no longer laughing. The look on his face indicated he was somewhere between mentally adding the good doctor to his hit list and debating if he was really worth it. "Guess we weren't exactly your first picks for the job. Huh, doc?"

Dr. Jameson furrowed his brow, the arch of one raised slightly higher than the other. "Would you trust the integrity of time to a mobster's son and an ex-society member's daughter?"

Adelaide froze, the force of his words was like an upper-cut to her jaw. "What did you say?"

Dr. Jameson winced. "You didn't know?"

Adelaide bit her lip, feeling the sharp taste of iron on her tongue. "No."

Dr. Jameson hesitated before running a defeated hand over his features. "Your mother was a member of the Red Rose Society, many years ago. I guess if she was alive now, she would still be considered one, but not long before you were born, she cut ties—"

He was interrupted by a loud bang and corresponding shout. "Ow!"

For the first time since arriving in the bottom of the pit, Adelaide noticed a pair of worn, sneakered feet sticking out from beneath the metal of the time machine. They pushed off the floor, propelling the young man forward just enough for him to swing his head out and stand. Kolt rubbed at a spot near his temple. A dark streak, like one of his cousin's charcoal drawings, smudged his skin. He dropped his hand and wiped it on a towel, its original color long overtaken by a series of dark stains. "Sorry, I was going to announce myself but never really found the right moment."

Dr. Jameson tossed Adelaide's and Teo's files back on his desk. The breeze from their impact sent a few scraps of paper over the side, cascading to the floor. "What are you doing here, Kolt? Where's Mikaelson?"

Kolt shoved the rag in the pocket of his coveralls. "He's still recovering from the typhoid he picked up in Ancient Greece."

"Typhoid?" Adelaide blanched. "As in typhoid fever?"

Kolt nodded. "Yeah, but med says he's on the mend and should be fully recovered in no time. However, you're out a pilot until then."

If Mikaelson was the pilot, what did that make Kolt? Up until now, Adelaide hadn't seen him since the funeral and her delayed realization of his identity the night of the gala. She quirked her head as she tried to puzzle out how he fit here. When she had first met him again as an adult, he had been slinging drinks across the bar of the Red Rose Society's hidden club and playing ferryman to new Kindred. Now, he was fixing the time machine. "I thought you were a bartender."

Kolt smirked as the light in the room darkened his eyes to a deep jade. "Everyone needs a day job, and lucky for you that's the case because I just fixed the nav-converter. Mikaelson's current predicament aside, you won't be going anywhere until Charlie recalibrates it."

Dr. Jameson ran his hands down his lab coat, his fingers working at a thread-bare button as his lips pursed. His eyes flitted briefly behind Adelaide. She followed his gaze to the catwalk where two figures now stood at the railing, looking down on them below. One was Matriarch, her ringed fingers gripped tightly around the metal rail. The other was a man Adelaide didn't recognize. Beside Matriarch in her crisp pant-suit, the man looked severely underdressed in a loose cotton button up and boat shoes. Wind and sun had touched his thick, chestnut hair. The tan of his skin and slight stubble on his jaw suggested he spent most of his time on the beach or a yacht instead of here, hundreds of feet underground.

Matriarch leaned toward the man. Her lips moved with words Adelaide was too far away to catch. Though they were meant for him, the man seemed to only half hear them, his eyes trained on Adelaide as she met his gaze. Something in his look made her uneasy. It wasn't menacing or sly, but it held the hint of something she couldn't place.

Adelaide pulled her gaze away. "Who's the man with Matriarch?"

Kolt glanced up as if just noticing them. "That's Gideon Hargrove."

Hargrove. It wasn't a name Adelaide had heard in a while, but it was one as familiar to her as her own. "My mother's maiden name was Hargrove."

"It was, indeed, Ms. Anson." Dr. Jameson dropped his hands, though they remained in fists at his side. "Their surname is one and the same. That man is her brother."

5

THE GIRL IN THE TOWER

The ride back up was as silent as the descent, though this time, Adelaide didn't mind. Between learning her mother had been a member of the Red Rose Society and seeing her uncle for the first time in over a decade, she welcomed the brief moment to process the information. Or at least try to.

Dr. Jameson had still been talking to them when Gideon slipped out of the room with Matriarch, so Adelaide hadn't gotten a chance to confront him. But even if she had, she wasn't so sure she wanted to. Whoever Gideon was now, he wasn't the man she had known. They may share the same blood, but over the years he had become a stranger. When she did talk to him, *if* she did talk to him, it would be for her mother's sake, not her own.

How could she not have known? Sure, admitting to your daughter that you had been in a secret society of historical descendants probably wasn't the easiest conversation to start. But the more Adelaide thought about it, the more it seemed to make sense. Her mother had been a researcher, a historian for hire to top-tier universities, organizations, and individuals who needed someone to dig into the past for them. Her mother had loved the unpredictability of the task and excitement of discovering something new from the past in her work. But the one thing she loved to do more than anything was genealogy, tracing family lines and mapping family trees. Knowing what Adelaide did now, it wasn't that big of a leap to consider that if her mother had been a member of the Red Rose Society, they must have been the ones to teach her.

But why hide it?

Adelaide felt like she had at five years old, doing puzzles with her uncle on the back porch. The pieces were large, the desired outcome clearly defined by the picture on the box, but still she couldn't quite fit them together. Usually because the puzzle was old and pieces were missing. The truth teased just out of reach. Until it came close enough to grab, close enough to take on solid form instead of floating through her mind in pieces as disjointed as her traces, she would keep digging.

While Adelaide knew the reason for her silence, she wasn't sure why Teo remained quiet too. Though she guessed it had to do with Barrow's death. The actual extent of their relationship was still a mystery to her, but whatever it was, it had been enough for her death to shake him. Teo seemed the type to never let a crack show in his polished façade, despite the things he must have witnessed growing up as he did, the son of a notorious mobster. Adelaide might have missed it, the false bravado, introspection and eyes dimmed by pain, if she hadn't known the kind of loss that held such power. Despite the arguments and anger she had witnessed back in the French Revolution, Barrow had meant something to him. Of that much she was certain.

Teo leaned back against the elevator wall across from her and hooked his thumbs in his pockets. No quippy remarks or imposing questions peppered the air, despite having an arsenal of new information to draw from. She could feel him watching her, words teased on his lips as he ran them over his palate as if deciding whether to swallow them or spit them out. He shifted on the wall and spat them out. "Where's your head at, Dollface?"

It was sweet of him to ask and not at all what she had expected him to say. But between the loss of her parents and Xander cutting her out the way he had, Adelaide had spent the last year building a wall of bricks around her heart. Teo's question felt too close to one that could topple them all. "What? Are we talking now?"

His eyes narrowed as he rolled his shoulders back. "I guess not, but from what I just heard it sounds like your family is even more screwed up than mine. Forget I asked."

Adelaide massaged her temple, wishing she could take back the words. She'd become accustomed to pushing others away for the sake of her heart, but more often than not, it was at the expense of it. How many times could you push a person away before they decided it was easier to give up on you than tear down the wall?

Adelaide knew she was in the wrong, but she didn't have the right words. And as the elevator stopped at her floor, it was easier to slip through and leave Teo inside than risk letting her walls crumble. Finding the portrait of Elizabeth I, she turned down the hall adjacent to it that led to the living quarters. She should be headed to the library. Dr. Jameson had instructed her to do some research on World War II before they reconvened in a few days when the time machine was fixed. But the last thing she wanted to do was read a book right now.

Adelaide passed the rooms of the other Kindred. She had learned they would live within these walls until the Red Rose Society determined they were ready to place on assignment. After that, they could find themselves anywhere in the world, preserving the past, protecting the present, and forging the future. Isn't that what she wanted to do as a historian? So what if a stepping stone on that path was training within the Red Rose Society? Sure, initiating Kindred the way they did with a test in time might not be the most ethical way to go about swearing in new members, but Juniper said scouts had been watching. They would have stepped in if they thought any of the initiates were in real danger. Right?

Then how come Barrow and Jonas are dead? Their names echoed in her head. She could still see the blood blossom across Barrow's chest like a rose, see Jonas' lifeless eyes staring up at the ceiling of the coliseum. *Who was protecting them?*

She made her way to the door at the back of the hall. Someone had carved roses into the dark wooden frame around it. A cherry stain dusted their polished petals with a hint of red. A rusted keyhole sat flush to the door, but instead of inserting a metal key, Adelaide waved the rose ring she'd been gifted at the gala over the scanner inside. The lock clicked, and she bumped the door open with her hip. The door gave way to a set of spiral stairs ascending to a small but neat room in a turret of the castle.

Charlie had tried to explain to her the technology behind it all, how on the outside, the building of the Red Rose Society's headquarters looked like a set of dilapidated ruins, but in actuality, had been rebuilt according to the original designs and masked by some expensive tech and a trick of light. But Adelaide could do little other than nod to show she was paying attention, only half understanding what Charlie was saying. Try as she might, her brain was hard-wired for history, literature, and art. Numbers and equations were as foreign to her as ancient runes or alchemy.

Adelaide sighed, relieved to find the room empty. Though she didn't necessarily mind Elise's company, she was glad to have a few moments to herself, especially after everything she had just learned. She flopped on her bed, not bothering to remove her high-tops, and stared up at the ceiling trying to remember the last time she had seen her uncle. The most recent memory she could conjure was her seventh birthday party. His arms had circled her waist and lifted her up to reach the piñata which took her nearly five swings to finally break and send a cascade of candy, like sugared rain, to the spring grass. She recalled his photo on the piano and post cards on the fridge telling stories of daring adventures and promises to visit soon. But since that day, he remained absent from her memory, and his figure slowly faded to the background as the years passed.

Thoughts of her uncle slowly morphed into thoughts of her parents. In the aftermath of the fire, Adelaide had mourned the loss of the big moments to come—graduations without them in the crowd, a walk down the aisle without her father beside her, the grandchildren her mother would never be able to hold. Their absence in those future moments still broke her heart, but in the days since, she had found herself missing more of the small moments, like a cold winter's night not long ago.

She'd tiptoed downstairs for a glass of water. Her feet carefully fell on the wooden floorboards in the same manner they had when she was young and trying to sneak around the house undetected. Despite the late hour, her mother was awake and scrawling in a journal as a fire sparked in the grate and threw shadows across her face. The fire darkened the already deep red leather of the cover to near black. The journal had been a Christmas gift from Adelaide, a new, blank canvas for her mother to fill with stories, both real and make-believe. Sensing her presence in the way only mothers can, she had set her journal down and moved to the side before throwing the blanket wide so Adelaide could squeeze in beside her. They sat that way for hours, moving comfortably in and out of conversation and silence until sleep claimed them both.

The irony of mundane moments is you don't see their beauty until they only exist in memory. With time, even that begins to fade. Adelaide tried to take comfort in the fact that her mother still existed on paper, that her words remained behind even if she could no longer speak them herself, but how do you sum up the whole of a person in twenty-six little letters. It didn't seem like enough.

Adelaide shifted her eyes to the foot of her bed. The room had been sparse when she and Elise were assigned to it. The only real items, aside from the staple bits of bedroom furniture, were a few odds and ends left behind from whoever lived there last; a thick woolen sweater, a ticket stub from an indie concert at a local coffee shop, and a worn copy of *The Great Gatsby* with the initials S.B. imprinted in gold foil on the cover. Though it didn't seem likely, there was still the possibility whoever the items belonged to would come back for them. It had seemed wrong to throw them away, so she'd piled them up beneath her bed for safe keeping.

Her own belongings had arrived a few days earlier. Of the little she owned, most was still back in America, save for the carry-on she had packed for the plane ride to Scotland. But a few boxes of clothes and books, along with her mother's trunk, had made the long flight over. The trunk now sat at the foot of her bed. She still hadn't been able to get herself to open it, or more importantly, read through any of her mother's journals inside. She sat up suddenly as a thought fluttered through her mind. Was there a chance her mother had written about the Red Rose Society?

Before her brain could catch up with her feet, Adelaide found herself kneeling in front of the trunk and lifting the latch. The familiar scent of worn leather and ink that had clung to her mother like perfume hit her as she eased the top open. Suddenly, she was a kid again, curled up in bed with her mother's cardigan draped over her shoulders. Its weight and scent were a comforting shield against bad dreams and monsters in the dark. Her hands moved on their own accord, aching to clasp these few remaining bits of her mother and glean all she could from the pages, but as if she were hit by an electric shock, she recoiled her hands. What would happen if she touched them? While the journals still called to her, it wasn't in the same way as the other objects that had catalyzed a *trace*. Mixed as her emotions were at the possibility of seeing her mother again, even in disjointed scraps, Adelaide knew she would have to open the journals eventually.

She dropped her hand and let her fingertips graze the embossing on the top cover. Her mind remained void of images, other than the ones Adelaide conjured herself. She wasn't sure if she was disappointed or relieved in the absence of a *trace* as each journal passed through her hands. She had forgotten how beautiful they were, all of them handcrafted and most of them purchased from a quaint little shop just outside of their countryside town. Journals were one of the few things she could remember her mother splurging on. When Adelaide had pointed that out to her, she had simply said, "a weapon as powerful as words must be properly sheathed like a sharpened sword."

She lifted one from the trunk and took a shaky breath before cracking open the pages. A tear slipped down her cheek as she ran her eyes along the familiar looping scrawl of her mother's handwriting. Unlike her father's heavy, messy script, which had been crammed together so tightly it looked as if each individual letter was in a race to surpass the other, her mother's was neat and light. Though the pages of the journal were unlined, a few centimeters of white above and below her words acted as a buffer between them. The entry Adelaide had opened to was dated back to her middle school days. She read a few other entries, most of which had covered quirky things Adelaide had said and done, family vacations they had taken or projects her mother was working on. She closed the journal, intending to finish it later, but she wanted to read something more recent. She rifled through the trunk, searching for the dark red leather of the journal she had given her mother on her last Christmas, but after checking and double-checking the volumes, she still couldn't find it among the others.

Adelaide was about to go through them a third time when footsteps sounded on the stairway. She looked up from the trunk, a journal in hand, just as Elise stepped through the door. A pile of books spilled from her arms as she peeked around the stack at Adelaide.

"Hey, Ad." Elise tossed the books on the bed opposite of Adelaide's and dropped down beside them. The pale pink rouching of her skater skirt bunched beneath her as she shimmied out of her boots.

Adelaide wasn't sure when they had crossed the threshold of familiarity that made Elise feel comfortable calling her "Ad" and not Adelaide, but given the fact the girl had saved her life more than once back in the French Revolution, she didn't correct her.

"What have you got there?" Elise kicked her boots to the side and came to stand beside Adelaide, peering over her shoulder at the contents of the trunk.

"My mother's journals. I was looking for one in particular, but it doesn't look like it ever made it into the trunk." She placed the one in her hand back inside, shut the lid, and sat on top.

"You lost them. Didn't you? In a house fire?" Elise, empathy clear on her face, sat back on the foot of her bed.

Adelaide wasn't sure how Elise knew about the fire, though with her eidetic memory she supposed the girl could have read about it somewhere and only recently connected her name to the article. Not trusting herself to speak with the fresh set of emotions her mother's words had brought to the surface, she simply nodded.

Adelaide gripped the trunk on either side of her and bit her lip. "What's with the books?"

Elise didn't push her, taking the change of subject in stride. "Juniper wanted me to start by learning the history of the Red Rose Society, so she sent me back with some books to read up on before we meet again."

Adelaide still hadn't gotten the chance to speak with Juniper privately. She supposed she could have asked Charlie or Xander how the woman fit in here as they had both known her outside of the Red Rose Society, but she wanted to hear it straight from her. While Juniper and her parents hadn't necessarily been close, the woman had always existed in the peripheral of Adelaide's life. It wasn't until the fire that she really became a central presence, hiring Adelaide at her diner, helping her find an apartment, checking in on her with a doggie bag of food and a cheesy romcom to divert her mind from the rift that had opened up in her world.

When they had been divided and assigned jobs, part of her had hoped she would get to apprentice under Juniper and train in the position Elise was now learning. At least then she would have had an excuse for asking questions and digging in places she wasn't supposed to. But given she was a Timewalker, whatever that really meant, she would have to be a little creative with how she searched for the truth. If she couldn't be a Keeper in training, having a roommate that was served as the next best thing.

"What do you know about the Red Rose Society? My invitation didn't exactly come with a detailed description of what I was getting myself into."

Elise pursed her lips. "Admittedly, probably not much more than you. To be honest, I'm not quite sure how they even found out about me, but my best guess is Colden. The auctions and parties his work throws attract quite an interesting array of people. I've been to several and would bet my ballet slippers at least one of them had a Red Rose Society member in attendance."

"Do you think Colden knows more about them?" She had a hard time believing he was oblivious to the kind of clientele his work associated with. Then again, her two best friends and her mother had been knee deep in the Red Rose Society and she hadn't had a clue.

"I don't think so." Elise shook her head. "Colden does the wining and dining, but all of his clients either find him or are hand-picked from a master list. If they were there, it wasn't because he invited them."

Colden might not know who among the guests of his openings and parties were Red Rose Society members, but that didn't mean he didn't know any. "Do you know who makes the list?"

Elise shrugged. "Probably someone at the auction house, but I couldn't tell you who."

If neither Elise or Colden knew much about the Red Rose Society, why did they show up at the gala at all? It had to be more than curiosity. If it hadn't been for the newspaper clipping of the fire that came with her invitation to the Red Rose Society, Adelaide wasn't sure she would have batted an eye at the letter. "Did anything else come with your letter?"

"What do you mean?"

"Did they," she cocked her head, trying to figure out how to phrase the rest of her sentence, "promise you anything?"

A shadow passed across Elise's eyes.

"They did. Didn't they? What was it?"

Elise bit her lip, weighing her words. "I've been dancing all my life, but a few years ago, I broke my ankle. Several surgeries later and it still isn't the same as it was. The only chance I have of ever dancing on stage professionally again is an experimental surgery far more expensive than what I can afford. And the waiting list for it is already pages long. I'll be aged out unless someone pulls some strings."

"And the Red Rose Society promised to do that, to bump you up the list?"

Elise ran the fabric of her comforter through her fingers, unable to meet Adelaide's eyes. "All the way to the top. Ballet is in my blood. It's the only future I've ever planned for myself, the only constant in my life other than Colden and his parents. Without it, I'm not sure what I am."

Though she was about as graceful as a peg-legged duck, Adelaide could understand where Elise was coming from. History wasn't necessarily something she could lose, but she would be equally as crushed if her dreams of pursuing it were derailed. It was an inherent part of her she couldn't remove without taking pieces of herself with it.

"What about you?" Elise questioned, finally meeting her gaze. "What did they promise you?"

"Answers."

6

JUMP SCARE

Adelaide wished she had a map to help her navigate the network of hallways that made up the Red Rose Society. At this point, she would even settle for a ball of yarn like the one Theseus used to escape the labyrinth. It was one thing to wander the halls at night, the whispers in the walls like notes in a song guiding her. But day was a whole other story. She stuck to the middle of the cobblestone paths, hands in the pockets of her cardigan to keep them from straying too close to the stone. Still, she could feel their pull like magnets eager to collide.

How hard could it be to find the library? Adelaide thought. She passed the suit of armor and hidden door beside it for the third time. Fairly certain she had gone left the last few tries, she veered right and nearly collided with a figure. She stuttered to a halt as the girl in front of her gasped and threw a hand over her chest.

"Gosh, Adelaide." Teddy chuckled as her breathing returned to normal. "What are you doing creeping around corners like that? You'll scare a person half to death."

Adelaide smiled, relieved to see a friendly face. "Says the girl whose favorite part of a horror movie is the jump-scare."

Teddy dropped her hand, her arms coming up to wrap around Adelaide. She squeezed the girl back. She could still remember when Teddy was born, had babysat for her when she was young and took the same amount of pride in her and her accomplishments as if she was her own flesh and blood. Though she was Charlie's little sister, Adelaide had grown to think of her as something akin to the sibling she'd never had.

Teddy released her with a wry smile on her face. "I like watching them, not living them. There's a difference. I'm glad I ran into you though. Charlie's looking for you."

"Did she say why?"

Teddy shook her head. The strands of her dirty blonde lob brushed her shoulders, swaying with the lace of the boho dress that draped on her frame. "Dunno, she wouldn't tell me. But she had that crazy look in her eyes she gets when she's either stumped or on the verge of a breakthrough."

Adelaide knew that look well. "The one where her eyes narrow and she bites the side of her tongue?"

Teddy quirked her face, trying to contort it like her sister. "Yeah, that's the one."

"Sounds serious. Where is she?"

"In the tech lab." Teddy pointed behind her and to the left, down a small hallway lined with invention patents in gold frames. "You can't miss it. Oh, and the password is ten thirty-one. But you didn't hear that from me." Teddy winked and rounded the corner as Adelaide headed off in the opposite direction. Looked like the library would have to wait.

She followed the passage to a bend in the hall that narrowed like the tip of a funnel. Her stomach clenched as she wondered what Charlie wanted to talk to her about. She remembered what Xander had said back in the French Revolution about asking Charlie to do some digging into the fire. Had she found something?

The hallway slipped slowly from ancient to modern. Oak doors gave way to ones made of smooth metal. Scanners and keypads replaced rusted locks and keyholes. She read the labels on the doors as she passed, *Data Storage, Harvey Jameson, PhD., Communications*, until she reached a large bank vault door labeled *Tech Lab*. A three-pronged twist handle sat at its center. Adelaide typed the code Teddy had given her into the keypad and yanked on the handle. She felt the gears give way as the lock clicked open.

The room was an odd blend, somewhere between a warehouse, a gym and a computer lab. Shelves extended to the right in endless rows, piled high with tech and other objects in various stages of completion. Too bright lights buzzed overhead, casting the scene below in a white glow that reminded Adelaide of a hospital. The far wall sported a series of targets, reminiscent of those used at a shooting range. Grouped in front of the wall was a variety of different equipment ranging from a foam pit to a small bike ramp and a clear cylindrical tube big enough to hold a human. A conglomerate of computers and other machines sat to the left. Some looked similar to the ones she had seen in the basement stationed around the time machine.

A small group of people huddled near the computers. Sam, Thomas Jefferson's descendant, sat at a monitor. Charlie, her hand braced on the back of his chair, leaned over his shoulder, peering at the screen. Cleopatra's descendant, Asena, stood in front of them. She fiddled with something in her ear as she glared at Adelaide across the room.

Adelaide swallowed, her throat still colored in bruises from her and Asena's fight for the earrings on the scaffolding. Though she had still received a place within the Red Rose Society, Asena didn't seem all that keen on forgetting Adelaide had beaten her.

Charlie spotted her and waved her over. "Ad, perfect. Say something in Latin for me."

"*Veritas numquam perit.*"

Charlie looked to Asena who shook her head.

"One more time."

Adelaide obliged. She was long past questioning Charlie's random, albeit strange requests. More often than not, she had a good reason for them. At least most of the time.

Charlie glanced back at Asena, but her response was the same. Dislodging something from her ear, she walked toward them and dropped it in Charlie's hand. It was small and clear, about the size of a dime. "Add Latin to the list. I don't know how often it'll be needed, but I guess it can't hurt."

"List of what?" Adelaide peered at the object. "What is that?"

Charlie beamed, her words tripping over each other the way they did when she was excited. "It's a prototype for a translation matrix. When it's ready, the Timewalkers will be able to understand and communicate back with those in any time period they jump to. It's still got some kinks, but I think we can get it operating with most of the common languages by the end of the year."

"That's actually really neat. Knowing you, I'm sure it'll be bug-free and halfway to ancient Macedonia before you know it." Adelaide only wished they'd had the device during the French Revolution. Maybe then she could have understood what the woman in the alley's last words had been. She shook the memory from her mind the best she could, but it lingered at the edge like the faded colors of a firework.

"Thanks, I hope so." Charlie turned to Sam and Asena. "You guys can go ahead and call it a day. I'll meet you back here tomorrow."

After Sam and Asena had left, Adelaide followed Charlie down a row of the shelves. Their metal structure climbed high above them, causing Adelaide to wonder how they managed to get to the objects at the very top or place them there to begin with. It felt like walking through the stone valleys carved straight from the earth that her father had hiked through to reach many of his dig sites. She had followed close behind him, her eyes everywhere trying to take it all in at once, but there was always so much to see that she didn't know where to look first. Charlie stopped short and read the label on the shelf below a square-shaped object about the size of a mini-fridge. She opened it and placed the translator inside while her fingers found a holographic keyboard projected from the box, which she proceeded to type on.

"Should I pretend I didn't see that?"

Charlie shut the door and watched the keypad disappear before turning to Adelaide. "Considering you're not technically supposed to be in here, probably." She leaned against a shelf and crossed her arms. "How did you get through the door anyway?"

"I ran into Teddy in the hall. She said you were looking for me?"

"Yeah…" Charlie said with the spark of something undiscernible in her eyes. "Every year the Red Rose Society hosts an auction. Aside from the Ancestral Gala, it's one of the biggest events of the year. Society members from every branch all over the world attend. It's a real who's who event, and this year, Matriarch's agreed to let me host it and donate half the proceeds to Harvard's Center for Marine Biology. I wanted to see if you would help."

"Sure." Adelaide tried not to let her disappointment show. Charlie's request wasn't anywhere close to what she'd thought her friend had wanted to tell her, but maybe she could use it to her advantage. "What do you mean members from every branch? I thought this was the Red Rose Society." Adelaide gestured to the building around them.

"It is. Edinburgh's branch is the main headquarters, but other branches just like this one are all over the world. The only real difference is that we have the only time machine. That I know of, at least. I've always suspected France has one too, but I've never been able to prove it."

If the Red Rose Society consisted of multiple branches and was as widely connected as Charlie had suggested, things just got a whole lot more complicated. Up until now, Adelaide had been operating under the assumption that whoever sent her the letter was here in Edinburgh, but they could be anyone from anywhere. She thought back to the gala, trying to single out faces in the crowd, but everything had happened so fast from the moment they jumped to the moment they returned that individual faces were all a blur. "What about Matriarch? Is she in charge of the whole thing or just this branch?"

"Every branch has a head in charge of the operations of their specific location, but together, along with a few other miscellaneous members, like Juniper and Xander's dad, they also make up a larger council called the Enclave. Matriarch is the head of both."

There it was again—Juniper's name. It seemed no matter where she turned or what she learned, the woman was the thread that connected it all. But what was the full picture? "Was that all?"

Charlie bit the side of her tongue and let out a breath. "No, but not here." She pulled her cell from her pocket and hit a number. "Hey, I've got Ad with me. Can you meet us in your studio in five? There's something I have to show you."

7

THERE'S ALWAYS A TRAIL

———

Adelaide found herself back in the hidden wing. Though it was midday, darkness clung to the room like cobwebs. Embers still glowed orange in the grate, but it had been hours since a roaring fire permeated the room with warmth. Charlie lit a few candles, their gentle flickers of light fighting to reach the shadows collected like dust in the corners. Adelaide watched the dancing flames as each sprang to life under Charlie's fingertips. Fire would always be to her one of those things with equal power to awe and horrify. The spark of a single flame on a cold night was enough to save a life or end it.

Xander's painting was still in progress. A wooden artist's palette caked in oil paint lay beside it on the stool. The peaks and valleys in the dried and blended colors were a work of art all their own. A few layers of blue in the waves added a depth to the sea that hadn't been there hours earlier.

The door creaked open, and Xander entered, a slight flush to his cheeks. He ran a hand through his hair and took a shaky breath. His free hand worked loose the top button of his starched white button-up. Shadows darkened his eyes to deep brown, leaving no hint of the gold Adelaide knew was there.

"Xander, what's wrong?" Adelaide thought it, but Charlie voiced it out loud as she crossed the room to lay a hand on Xander's arm. They had always been close, and Charlie clearly meant it as a means of comfort, but an intimacy in the touch made Adelaide wonder if it wasn't something more.

Xander laughed once, a dry and brittle chuckle escaping his lips. "Well, I just left my father and grandmother arguing, if that answers your question at all."

"About what?" Her voice drew his eyes to Adelaide, as if he had only just realized she was in the room.

"Doesn't matter." It did, and they all knew it, but they also knew enough to know they couldn't push him. He would tell them what was going on when he found the way to turn his art to words. "What did you find, Charlie?"

Charlie didn't look satisfied with his answer, but she didn't push him on it either. Seeing the only furniture in the room was the stool, she took a seat on the floor in front of the fireplace and motioned for them to do the same. They obliged, dropping beside her as she opened the laptop they had grabbed from her room on the way over.

"I'm not entirely sure yet," Charlie said as she focused on the screen. "Xander told me about your conversation, that something about the fire wasn't sitting right with you. So, I started doing some digging." She turned the laptop toward them.

Adelaide ran her eyes along the screen. On it was what looked like a redacted police report. Thick, black lines of ink overed most of the text. The only words visible, other than the date and location at the top of the document, were the ones Adelaide had repeated to herself over and over since that day: her parents' names, *fire*, and *accident*.

Adelaide's stomach dropped. "I could have shown you this, Charlie. Sheriff Dawson gave me a copy. It's somewhere in my notebook." She had hoped Charlie might have actually found something useful, but she knew the police report front to back. The only way she would be able to learn more from it was if she could scrub the black ink off and reveal the words beneath the censored pieces, but that wasn't an option. She had tried.

"I know, but this one, the one you have, isn't copied from the original report." She pulled up another window, placing a second document beside the first.

At first glance, they looked the same, but when Adelaide looked closer, she could see the first report was shorter than the second. "I don't understand. Why are there two of them?"

"I wanted to see if I could find a scan of the original report, unredacted, so I broke the firewall to the Atkin County records. This second report, the one Sheriff Dawson gave to you, is the one they have on file for the night of the fire, but after some more digging, I found this other one with an earlier scan date. Someone tried to delete it, but nothing is ever as gone as we think it is. There's always a trail if you know where to look."

"And you found it. But why delete the original and swap the files?" Adelaide's heart raced, suspecting she already knew the answer.

Charlie worried a curl between her fingers. "I wasn't able to fully redact the original document, but I did find a reference to a foreign piece of DNA at the crime scene. Whoever removed that information and scanned in the fake report clearly didn't want anyone to know about it. Now, it could mean nothing, but if we were able to connect the DNA to a person and actually place them at the crime scene, we could have a witness."

Adelaide brushed her curls back and let out the breath she was holding. It wasn't the whole truth, but at least it proved she wasn't crazy. Someone out there held the answers she was looking for, but who?

8

THE RULES OF TIME

———

Bookshelves blurred around Adelaide in a haze of leather, parchment, and ink as she blazed past them. The once-comforting smell of vanilla-aged paper was now a bittersweet aftertaste of memories she desperately wanted to both forget and cling to in equal measure. She should be happy Charlie found a clue, and in a way, she was. It was in no way a complete answer to her questions. If anything, it posed another altogether. But it also offered a sliver of hope Adelaide hadn't felt in quite a while that helped her believe maybe she wasn't a crazy, grief-stricken child like Sheriff Dawson and many others believed. She was a grieving daughter seeking closure no one could or would willingly provide. So she'd have to find it herself.

For all she knew, the DNA could be nothing. It could have been left behind by one of her father's colleagues or just an unfortunate mix-up at the lab. But if that was the case, why would someone go to the trouble of hiding it? She was missing something. She might not know what yet, but she did know where to start digging.

Adelaide raised her wrist and rapped on the oak door at the back of the library. Juniper's voice beckoned her in from the other side. Incense perfumed the air, melding with Juniper's lavender and moss scent that eased the tension in Adelaide's shoulders. The woman sat at her desk, books open and stacked around her like a fortress. Adelaide tried to catch a glimpse of the titles, but each was written in a different language. Greek, Hebrew, French and a mix of others glinted gold on the worn, leather spines.

Juniper, her gloved hands gently turning the page of a particularly brittle book, looked up as Adelaide approached. "Hey, sugar. I was wondering when you'd stop in. What brings you by?"

Adelaide dropped into the velvet-lined chair opposite Juniper's. As she did, her hand grazed the edge of a book on the woman's desk, and she caught a glimpse of a red-headed girl in a wedding dress. She shook the *trace* off, her eyes darting to Juniper, but the woman showed no sign of having seen anything out of the ordinary.

Several questions stirred in Adelaide's mind—about her mother and her uncle—but she found her thoughts centered on Matriarch and the man in the hallway. Their conversation had played in her head since that night. It folded over itself like origami. But no matter how many ways she spun it, it always brought her back to the same question. "When I brought the earring back at the gala, has anything like that ever happened before?"

Juniper removed her gloves and tossed them on her desk. Something like recognition flitted in her eyes, quickly replaced by a dazed expression. "Time is a fickle thing. It easily bends but very seldom breaks. What you did at the gala breaks all the rules of time we thought we knew."

Adelaide could still feel the bite of the earring in her bloody palm, its weight a lifeline she hadn't wanted to drop. "Breaks them how?"

Juniper pursed her lips and pushed a loose curl aside. "Actual time travel works a lot differently from how film and books portray it. You can't just jump to any time and place you want. It has to be a 'hot zone,' a place so chaotic and volatile that the presence of, say, a few Kindred or a group of Timewalkers won't cause much of a dead wake."

That would explain why Adelaide and the other Kindred had been sent to the French Revolution. Between the political upheaval and the violence rife in the streets, enough unpredictability kept their actions in check. "What do you mean by a dead wake?"

"The ripples left behind when someone returns from the past. Actions and reactions, just like in the present, cause a ripple effect. It's impossible to time travel and not cause a ripple, but small ripples in a hot zone are reset by the timeline, leaving very little impact."

Adelaide wasn't entirely sure she understood all of what Juniper had said, but she got the gist of it. "So, history repeats itself and has a built-in buffer system to keep the actions of any time travelers from affecting the timeline as it stands?"

"Exactly," Juniper absentmindedly traced circles on her desk with her finger. "It's not a perfect system. Some actions still cause ripples the time barriers can't contain, but for the most part, the moment someone returns, history acts like they were never really there. It's part of the reason items crumble outside of their timeline."

History might forget, but Adelaide knew she wouldn't any time soon. She could still hear the woman's scream from the alley echoing in her dreams. Some experiences couldn't be forgotten no matter how far removed you were from them. She knew that better than anyone, and while it had given her a bit of comfort knowing there was little they could do to actually screw up the timeline, she wasn't so sure that was true anymore. "So, what does it mean? The fact that I can bring things back?"

Juniper's finger stopped twirling on her dust-free desktop as she cast a glance at her books. "It means all bets are off and all those things we didn't believe possible might just be. Because of you."

9

TRACES

———

APRIL 24, 1558
FRANCE

France in April was a medley of weather—a mix of seasons all shoved into a single month, which chose day by day what it wanted to be. Warm days of sun would break life through the soil as the early buds of spring reached toward the light, only to turn cold with an unforgiving frost that robbed the land of life. Many visitors to the country and even natives of the French court found themselves at odds with the fickle weather, but not Mary. She reveled in its unpredictability, its unrestrained freedom to be any and all it wanted to be.

One night, not long after her arrival at court, she watched the beginnings of an April snowfall through her window. Fat, crystalline flakes blanketed the ground in a fresh coat of white that washed the world of color. When the palace grew quiet, Mary had rushed downstairs with her ladies, the five of them donning boots and furs as they snuck silently past the guards and out into the dark of night. She'd gasped as the crisp air hit her skin, a laugh escaping her lips as she sank into the snow. Mary had closed her eyes, losing herself in the glide of her limbs over the fresh powder and the nearness of her friends beside her imprinting angels in the snow. Only when they lingered just a little too long did they finally make their way back to the castle.

Though April snowfalls brought memories of her youth, Mary loved French weather most as it was now, fresh off a recent rainfall, the damp soil perfuming the air in an earthy musk that reminded her of Scotland. Despite the years that had passed since she had last breathed Scottish air, the smell lingered in her soul, rising to the surface of her memory any time it rained. It had drizzled on and off for the past couple of weeks. Heavy droplets fell from the sky and soaked into the earth right up until the moment Marie de Guise set foot in France. Her mother was never one for frills and parties, preferring to focus her time on battle strategies and political alliances, but for Marie, her daughter's marriage offered a unique opportunity to kill two birds with one stone. Her mother had been waiting a lifetime for this moment and now, it was finally here.

For all her time in France, Mary had never seen the streets as lively as they were today. Throngs of people lined the cobblestone, filling every inch of available space on either side of the marked path through the city. They swayed like wheat in a field as they jostled one another for a better view of the scene. Those who couldn't find purchase on the ground climbed on roofs and leaned out the second-story windows of bars and inns with eyes trained on the processional weaving its way through the dense crowd. They waved ribbons in their hands in celebration, all eager to lay eyes on the young dauphin and his bride as they made their way through the streets of Paris.

Mary spotted her mother as she crossed the worn steps of the cathedral, the woman's face a mask except for the slight dip at the corner of her mouth. She locked eyes with Mary and inclined her head. Her mother was many things, but subtle was not one of them. Taking her cue, Mary straightened her back and tilted her chin to keep the crown on her head from slipping.

Mary learned early on the weight of a crown lay not in the jewels and precious metals that adorned it, but in the duty that came with it. A mere six days after her birth, her father died, leaving her the weight of a crown on her head and a kingdom at her feet before Mary had the chance to greet the world as anything else.

Minstrels in bright reds and yellows perfumed the air with song almost as overpowering as the oils and perfumes floating in a cloud around her. Banners hung on the walls, reminiscent of the ones flapping in the breeze on the windows of the houses and shops outside the cathedral. Their bold colors were like jewels against the grey of the stone buildings offering more than decoration for the occasion, but a promise. The red of their dye echoed the red of her blood that, in moments, would tie France not just to Scotland, but to the English crown.

Whispers of Elizabeth had followed Mary all her life, like a shadow she couldn't shake. Her English cousin now sat in a cell in the Tower of London, but it was no secret her current state might be soon fated to change. Rumors and whispers floated *about that Elizabeth's sister, England's current queen, was dying. Though Elizabeth was declared illegitimate by Parliament and at odds with her sister, England still needed an heir should their queen soon pass. Eyes had started to turn outward, and the Tudor blood that ran in her veins gave Mary a claim to England that rivaled her cousin's. She had never declared the country her own, but others were pushing for her to take the throne. The scales of England's fate could soon be tipping, and if Mary played her cards right, they could be in her favor.*

10

CHANGE OF PLANS

The time machine was finally fixed. At least that was what Adelaide hoped as she yawned and punched the elevator button for the basement. One of the techs from the lab had awakened her, along with Elise, and relayed it was time for their first jump. They had both already been back in time, but Adelaide supposed the gala didn't count. No matter the carnage they had seen, no matter the lives lost, the trip tallies didn't start until they were official members of the Red Rose Society.

The elevator doors opened, and Elise squinted against the light. "Ah! Did these people not get the memo that it's the middle of the night?" She held a hand up, trying and failing to block out the light. "Who time travels at this ungodly hour, anyway?"

"Apparently I do." Adelaide sighed, stepping onto the catwalk. "But I think I need to renegotiate my hours. I don't function properly between the hours of eleven and eight."

Elise dropped her hand in defeat. "You and me both, my friend."

They made their way to the apparatus floor. Techs buzzed about in lab coats and spectacles, pressing buttons and flipping switches in preparation for the jump. Instead of a series of numbers, the largest screen displayed a 3-D graphic of an oval, sketched out like a blueprint. Dr. Jameson, Juniper, and Teo were already there along with another man Adelaide hadn't seen before. He looked to be in his early- to mid-thirties, the faintest hint of grey salting his dark hair. Despite the lateness of the hour, his eyes gleamed with an excitement Adelaide wasn't sure she shared.

"Nice of you to join us, ladies." Dr. Jameson eyed them above his wire-rimmed glasses. "I know history is in the past, but that does not mean it will wait for us."

"Sorry," Adelaide said, sarcasm flavoring her words. "We figured we should at least stop to brush our teeth seeing as any time we're headed to probably doesn't have spearmint toothpaste."

Dr. Jameson nodded as if that was a decent enough excuse for their tardiness. "Very well," He gestured between Adelaide and Teo. "Mikaelson, show these two the storeroom while I get Juniper and Ms. Carroll up to speed."

"You got it, boss." Mikaelson saluted and turned on his heel.

He didn't look back to see if they were following. Adelaide met Teo's gaze and shrugged, taking off after Mikaelson.

Apparently he had fully recovered from typhoid fever because his pace was a near sprint, even for her long legs. He shot them a grin as they caught up and extended a hand. "Mikaelson."

"Nice to meet you," Adelaide said, grabbing his hand.

At the same time Teo said, "Yeah, I gathered that much."

Mikaelson ignored Teo and pushed open a thick metal door just off the apparatus floor. Cool air brushed Adelaide's skin as she crossed the threshold. She gasped, the sound quickly lost in the vast space. Rows of clothes from every era stretched before them. She ached to try them on and be somebody else from a whole other time, even if just for a day. To slip into a Victorian gown for a garden party, a forties-style swing dress for a night out dancing, a riding cloak for a midnight ride through a medieval countryside.

"Yeah." Mikaelson, a sly grin etching his face, watched Adelaide. "I was a theater kid growing up, so that was pretty much my reaction, too, when I saw this place for the first time." He rubbed his hands together. "Let's get you guys suited up."

"Alright," Teo pulled a twenties-style fedora from a rack and slipped it on his head. "But if it includes short pants and high socks, I'm out."

"Well," Mikaelson said, leading them down an aisle marked *1860s America*. "Lucky for you the pants have gotten a little longer from the last time period you jumped to."

Adelaide could think of only one reason for them to be looking through clothes from 1860s America, though she hoped for their sake she was wrong. "We're going back to the Civil War? I thought we were starting with World War II."

"Right you are, my dear. On both accounts." Mikaelson rifled through a rack, promptly piling up pants and jackets in Teo's arms. "There seems to have been a change in plans."

Teo peered over the growing pile. "Why?"

"Don't know, but Jameson will fill us in. For now, we need to get you properly dressed." Mikaelson threw a grey hat on top of the pile. "That should do it for the boys." Turning to Adelaide he added, "You're going to want to consult ERMA for your outfit."

"Erma?" Adelaide quirked her head. "I don't suppose she's a little old lady with a penchant for Civil War fashion?"

Mikaelson laughed. "Not quite, come on."

He led them deeper into the room to a small alcove in the far back corner. Four sets of curtains, two on either side of them, were tied back over the entrance of changing rooms. A pedestal stood in front of a large mirror, set into the center of the main wall.

"Go ahead." Mikaelson gestured to the pedestal. "Step up, keep your arms at your side and try not to move."

"Where's Erma?" Adelaide said, watching her reflection in the mirror.

"You're looking at her." Mikaelson said. "ERMA, be a dear and give Adelaide, here, a change of clothes. Classifications: Civil War, Richmond, Confederate, middle-class, female."

Adelaide watched as the mirror's surface rippled, giving way to a digital screen. The words Mikaelson had just spoken, classifications for the clothing she needed, scrawled across the upper left-hand corner as if typed by an invisible hand. The words finished typing, and a green beam emitted from the center of the mirror, coming to rest on her feet.

"Scanning," an electronic voice said, not unlike the one emitted from the disc that had given her and the other Kindred their instructions back in Revolutionary France. The beam slowly rose higher, creeping up every inch of her until she was face to face with a life-size, 3-D image of herself on the screen.

"Huh," Teo said, titling his head, an irritating smirk etched on his face. "I had you pegged as a boyshorts kind of girl."

She blushed, embarrassed on behalf of the model of her that was standing there in a black bra and underwear. Thankfully the image shifted as ERMA pulled up a queue of Civil War style dresses. Each one passed in front of the model, disappearing faster than Adelaide could register what they looked like. Finally, the dresses slowed like a gameshow wheel until a deep blue gown settled over the model's figure. Boxes like thought bubbles popped up on the dress, shoes, bag and brooch at the collar of the dress. Each listed a series of numbers and letters, presumably the location of each item in the warehouse.

"Thank you, ERMA. Upload those pieces and inventory coordinates to my phone please." Mikaelson extended a hand to help Adelaide off the pedestal. "Isn't she a doll?"

"Why ERMA?" Adelaide watched as the model faded and the reflective surface of the mirror rippled back into place.

"ERMA is short for ERa Module Apparel." Mikaelson beamed like a proud mother. "Took a few tries to get her right, but now, give her any combination of classifications, and she'll assemble a period-appropriate outfit for you in no time."

"You created her?"

"I did," Mikaelson said. "Though Charlie helped bring her to life. I told her my vision, and she wrote the code."

Though it wasn't her forte, Adelaide had always been amazed at what a series of zeroes and ones could do, especially in Charlie's hands. From the time they were little girls in pigtails, Charlie had been anything but what people expected from her. Like her idol Hedy Lamarr, she was beauty and brains in equal measure. Every bit an Old Hollywood starlet and scientist wrapped into one. She could build a computer from scraps and hack a database as quickly as she could turn a head and paint a nail.

Mikaelson's phone chimed, presumably with the information he'd requested from ERMA. He laid it flat in his palm and tapped the screen, bringing up a small hologram of the outfit and thought bubbles of the articles' locations within the warehouse. "Teo, you can go ahead and get changed. Adelaide, I'll be right back with your outfit."

Mikaelson headed back into the main portion of the warehouse, leaving her with Teo. He tossed the pile of clothes on a bench in one of the dressing rooms. "Try not to miss me," he said with a grin, sliding the curtain across the bar. He emerged a few minutes later with the grin wiped clean from his face. "Is it too late to back out now?"

Adelaide tried and failed to bite back a laugh. He looked like a man trying to play dress-up. His pants were a hair too short, the elbows on his jacket were worn, and a button near the top of his vest was missing.

Teo glared at her, but his outfit managed to take the edge off it. "What am I supposed to be, anyway?"

"An Italian immigrant looking for work," Mikaelson said, returning with a dress. "And you, my dear," he added a hand to his chest for dramatic flair, "are the war widow kind enough to hire him as you look to start over in the Confederate capital." He handed her the dress and a myriad of other accessories. "Put these on and meet us back on the apparatus floor when you're done."

Mikaelson ducked into the dressing room Teo had previously occupied, leaving Adelaide to slip into the one beside it. She shimmied on the inner layers, slipping into a light chemise and lacing a pair of heeled boots before adding the hoopskirt and the dress on top. It was a beautiful dress, made of a deep blue, almost black, cloth. Threads a shade lighter than the fabric formed patterns of leaves down the front and through the skirt. The sleeves were formfitting, but not tight, ending at the wrist in layered cuffs lined with ruffles. The back was lovely too, but there was one problem. It was corseted. She tried lacing it herself behind her back, but it was impossible to see if she was even looping the ribbon through the right slots.

"Dollface, what's taking so long? We could have been there and back by now." Teo's voice echoed through the warehouse.

"You ever try putting on a Civil War era dress? It's a little harder than slipping into a pair of tiny pants."

"Ouch." Teo laughed. "You really know how to wound a guy. What's the problem?"

Adelaide blew out a breath in defeat. She held an arm to her chest to keep the dress from slipping down and slid back the curtain. "I can't work the laces."

Teo swiped a thumb over his lips and walked toward her. His eyes shown even darker than normal in the dim lighting. "Turn around."

Adelaide turned, swiping her hair to the side and twisting her fingers in it as Teo's hands settled at the base of her back. Black licorice and smoke clung to him like a thick fog. She couldn't help but wonder as he tightened the ribbons if this was an odd change for him. Teo seemed more like the type to help a girl out of a dress than into one. She stifled a gasp as his cold fingers brushed the skin between her shoulders. He pulled his hands away and stepped back as if her skin had burned him.

Teo cleared his throat. "You should be good now."

"Thanks," she said, turning back around.

"Sure." Teo avoided her eyes, picking the cap up off the ground. He brushed past her, headed for the exit. "We should go."

"Annalise Bordeaux, Mateo Accardi, Robert Archer," Dr. Jameson said as he thrust manila folders into her, Teo, and Mikaelson's hands. "These are your aliases, at least for today. Memorize them, breathe life into them and when in doubt, make something up. But always remember your lies."

Adelaide opened her folder and scanned through its contents. *Annalise Bordeaux, twenty-three, widowed, librarian.* It wasn't much of an information overload, but definitely enough to make her wish she had some of Elise's eidetic memory. "How much time do we have?"

"About two minutes," Dr. Jameson said, checking his watch. "You'll usually receive these ahead of time, but this was a bit of an impromptu trip."

It had seemed odd to her they were jumping in the middle of the night, but she'd just chalked it up to the Red Rose Society wanting to make up for the trip they were supposed to take the first time. But if this trip wasn't planned, why the sudden urgency to get them to the Civil War?

"What should we do when we get there?" she asked.

"Thirty seconds!" a tech shouted, his voice barely discernible above the growing noise in the room.

"Hide the time machine," Dr. Jameson said, ushering them toward it.

Mikaelson was already seated, a head-set with an attached microphone over his ears and a hand on a joystick surrounded by multicolored buttons.

"Twenty seconds!"

"Find Elizabeth Van Lew and gain her trust," Dr. Jameson continued, helping her into the time machine behind Teo.

She tripped on the fabric of her hem, but a pair of hands settled on her waist, stopping her fall. Her head snapped up to Teo's, inches from her own. He looked away as she squeezed past him and dropped into her seat.

"Ten seconds!"

"Buckle up," Dr. Jameson said as the door slid shut.

Her hands shook, trying to snap the buckle in place.

"Five seconds!"

Teo eased the belt from her hands and clicked it in the lock.

The lights flickered and cut to black as a familiar buzzing sound crept into Adelaide's head.

"One!"

11

RICHMOND

JUNE 10, 1861
RICHMOND, VIRGINIA

A wave of warmth hit Adelaide as she stepped down on shaky legs feeling like a sailor returning from sea. Her heels sank into the soft earth with a squelch, evidence of a recent rainfall not yet dried from the summer heat. They were in a clearing of a small batch of trees, not quite a forest, but large enough to conceal them from wandering eyes. Sunlight filtered through the canopy overhead, making patterns of light and shadow dance on the ground. Warm wind whipped through the clearing, rustling the leaves and lifting Adelaide's curls. The faintest hint of gunpowder perfumed it with an undertone that told her they were far enough from the closest battlefield to be relatively safe but close enough for her senses to pick up on the evidence of it in sight, sound, and smell.

Mikaelson tapped at a panel on the side of the time machine and stepped back. Like the flicker of a dying bulb, it winked and faded from view, revealing a road behind it, just ahead through the trees. "That road will take us straight to Richmond," Mikaelson said, pointing beyond the trees to the faint shape of buildings in the distance.

They followed the road to the edge of the capital, where fields and farmland estates gave way to city streets and brick houses. Merchants with wooden carts lined the block, where they sold everything from fruit and pastries to cloth and dolls. Women in colored dresses trimmed in lace and men in Sunday suits and top hats bustled about, hopping from vendor to vendor as they filled the bags gripped in their palms with fruit and trinkets.

Adelaide found herself filled with the same odd mix of wonder and wrong she'd felt back in Paris. It was an indescribable thing to walk streets both familiar and foreign all at once. She could see Richmond as it had been in the past, laid out in the scene before her. Having been to the city in the present, she could also see how the passing years had chipped away at it like waves against stone. She stood there in awe, trying not to stick out like a tourist, but that's exactly how she felt in a time not her own and draped in clothes from a bygone era.

Her time in Paris had been filled with a sense of urgency. Between the threat of death around every corner and the ticking clock of the Red Rose Society's game, she hadn't been able to stand still and actually appreciate the wonder of where she was. The sights, the sounds, the colors, they brought history to life in a way she didn't know was possible, and the excitement of that experience alone was enough to thrill her.

She wanted to run her eyes over everything she could and imprint the image of the past on her mind in ink.

But underneath the thrill and excitement were reminders of the world she had walked into, a world divided in blue and grey, in black and white, in slave and free. She'd seen the slaves laboring in the fields on either side of the dirt road to the city. Their ebony skin glistened in the midday sun as they worked through a long hour of an even longer day. Adelaide knew there was more to the war than the argument of slavery, that state's rights, government authority and a slew of other things fueled the flames of a war that pitted brother against brother, father against son. While these were real questions of the time with real-world consequences, should either side prove victorious, their answers for both the North and the South had been put fully on the backs of the slaves. In them, the South saw a way of life, a cog in their wheel that was essential to their very survival. And while she believed many in the North had a true desire to end slavery, how many only saw emancipation as the best way to cripple the South and win the war?

"Move faster, girl," a woman's voice said, drawing Adelaide's attention to the crowd. She traced it back to a young woman in lace with cheeks rouged a deep pink. The woman walked to the next stand and began inspecting a jeweled necklace. A young black girl in braids, no more than eight years old, trailed behind her, arms piled high with bags and boxes as her little legs tried to keep up with her mistress. The blur of fur streaked past her as a dog ran between them. When the girl swerved to avoid it, the box at the peak of her little tower toppled to the ground and burst open, sending a cascade of silk and feathers straight into a puddle.

"You foolish girl!" the woman exclaimed. She grabbed her arm, and a small cry escaped from the girl's lips as the woman pulled her into an alley beside the jewelry booth.

Adelaide took a step toward where the two disappeared as her hand reached for the leather purse in which she had hidden Elise's dagger before the jump. A hand clasped her own arm, and Adelaide whipped around. Teo shook his head, a righteous anger in his eyes she was sure echoed her own. "We can't."

Adelaide nodded her understanding, biting her lip against the words she knew wouldn't make a difference. Teo, his face skewed as if his own words had left a bad taste in his mouth, let go. They were there to observe, record and report. Anything more outside of their mission parameters and they risked altering the timeline in ways they couldn't possibly predict. Even their best-intentioned actions could alter things, and who knew if it would be for the better.

She took a breath and ran her eyes around the market. A young boy stood a few feet from them with a thick stack of papers in his hands. Adelaide fished a coin from the leather purse and approached him. "I'd like a paper, please."

A bored expression on his face, the boy barely looked at her. He took the coin and slipped it into his pocket before handing over a newspaper. It was a copy of the *Richmond Dispatch*. Adelaide scanned the front page, reading the headline.

Nurses for the Army

A number of efficient nurses are required by the demands of the service to take proper care of the sick and invalid soldiers who are now contending for liberty against a worse than savage foe. Knowing the characteristic patriotism of our ladies, we believe on learning the above fact the question will be with them not who shall go, but who shall stay behind. Ladies who may feel interested in the subject can obtain all necessary information by calling on Mrs. A.F. Hopkins, at the American Hotel.

She flicked her eyes back to the top where the date read *June 10, 1861.* "Look at the date." Adelaide passed Teo the newspaper. "The war has been going on for less than two months, and Richmond's been the Confederate capital for even less than that."

No wonder the people in the market seemed relatively at ease, despite being in the midst of a war. It had barely even begun. They still thought it would be over soon, their sons and husbands back around the dining table before the end of the summer, their lives and loved ones untouched by the hardships of war. Little did they know this was just the beginning. Several years of loss and bloodshed lay ahead for the North and the South alike. No one would leave the war unscathed.

"Why now?" Teo arched a brow. "What's so important about today?"

"I'm not sure," Adelaide said, trying to recall what the war looked like at this point. "There's a battle today near Newport News, but that's several miles from Richmond. It must have something to do with Elizabeth Van Lew. She hardly ever leaves the city. What do you think Mikaelson—"

Adelaide turned to look over her shoulder, but the space beside them Mikaelson had previously occupied was vacant.

"Where'd he go?" Teo asked as the same question floated through her mind.

She swept her eyes over the crowd, turning every which way in search of his grey uniform, but still she saw no sign of him anywhere. A sense of panic welled in her chest. Neither she nor Teo knew how to pilot the time machine. If they couldn't find Mikaelson, how would they get back to their own time? After several more moments of searching, it was clear Mikaelson was not among them.

Suddenly, Adelaide's gaze connected with a figure several yards away. A look of recognition lit the girl's features, but she quickly hid it, turning her face and weaving deeper into the crowd.

It couldn't be, Adelaide thought. Without thinking, she took off after the girl. Teo yelled something as she pulled away, but his voice was already far enough behind her that it blended with the others in the market.

"Sorry!" Adelaide yelled as she collided with a woman. Food and other items tumbled with her bags to the ground.

If the woman said something back, Adelaide didn't hear it, her eyes tracking the girl in front of her as she quickened her pace and ducked into an alley. Adelaide did the same. She pulled up short, catching her breath as the walls on either side of her muffled the noise from the market. The alley ended at a solid brick wall, the only way out a wooden door on the right that led to the butcher's shop. Other than Adelaide, the alley remained empty. She ran to the door, testing the knob, but it was locked. The sign behind the glass read CLOSED in big black letters.

Adelaide rubbed her forehead. Despite the absence of the tell-tale ache in her head, she couldn't help but wonder if her eyes were playing tricks on her. Had the girl she saw even been real?

Teo burst into the alley with his gun drawn as he moved it around searching for a target. He lowered it slowly, his features relaxing as he realized there wasn't an immediate threat. The barrel glistened in the sun like a flash of a mirror held to light.

"Are you crazy? Put that away before someone sees." Adelaide gestured to the gun.

"Oh, I'm sorry," Teo clicked on the safety and slid the gun into a holster hidden beneath his jacket. "The next time I think you're in danger, I'll keep my gun holstered for the sake of history."

"I'm serious. Do you have any idea what could happen if a modern weapon falls into the wrong hands? Or even the right ones?"

"Have you ever shot a nineteenth-century pistol?"

"No." Truth be told, Adelaide had never even shot a modern one.

"Well I have, and let's just say that if we run into trouble, you'll be glad I broke the rules on this one."

Adelaide still didn't like it, but she knew there would be no convincing him otherwise. Until they returned to the present, she couldn't do anything about it. "Fine, just don't use it unless you absolutely have to."

"I never use it unless I absolutely have to," Teo said with a hard glint in his eyes. "But I'll watch my weapon as long as you agree not to run off again. What did you see anyway?"

"Nothing." Adelaide shook her head. But she could still see the girl, her chestnut waves and soft features plain as day in her mind... the same girl who had fired a shot at her in Paris.

12

OF SMOKE AND SHADOW

JUNE 10, 1861
RICHMOND, VIRGINIA

"Let's just do what we came to do and get out of here," Teo said as they gave up their search for Mikaelson. "He's got to make his way back to the ship eventually if he doesn't want to get stuck here. Right? We'll have to hope he's waiting when we get there."

"I guess…" Adelaide trailed off. But she could think of only two reasons they couldn't find him. Either Mikaelson was in trouble or he didn't want to be found. She wasn't sure which was worse—for him or for them.

"So, who is she, anyway?" Teo bit into an apple he'd swiped from a cart. "Elizabeth Van Lew?"

"She's a Union spy," Adelaide said, lowering her voice. "She runs the largest espionage network active during the Civil War. Nothing happens in Richmond without her knowing about it."

Teo munched on his apple with a quizzical look on his face. "So how do we find her?"

Adelaide knew that at this point in the war, Elizabeth's ring was in its early stages, but it was still wide-reaching. She'd been born and raised in Richmond, and her family had been active in the city's social circles for years. For all Adelaide knew, the fishmonger or the woman speaking with him could be one of her spies. Or the Confederates'.

Adelaide grabbed the brooch clasped at her neck, and an idea formed in her mind as her thumb grazed its surface. "Look for a clover."

"Pardon?" Teo tossed his core to the side.

"In order to identify each other, Elizabeth's network would carve three-leaf clovers out of peach pits and put them somewhere subtle but noticeable if you knew where to look. Like a watch chain or a pendant."

"Okay," Teo pushed off the wall he was leaning against. "You start from this end of the street, I'll start from the other, and we'll meet in the middle."

They split up, and Adelaide began her search. She tried to blend in, making small talk with the other patrons and purchasing small items here and there as she made her way toward the center of the market.

"Ma'am," Teo said, materializing beside her as she surveyed a spread of pastries at the baker's stall. "I believe I found what you're looking for."

Adelaide thanked the baker for her time and stepped off to the side with Teo. She wasn't too keen on him calling her ma'am but understood it was safer for them both if he did. She'd noticed more than a few eyes follow the two of them with a look of disapproval on their faces. To them, she was a Southern lady, and Teo was a foreigner getting a little too close. He led her to the storefront window of a tailor shop with a soft white gown displayed on the frame behind it. Teo swallowed, the dress silhouetted in his dark eyes as she watched him in the reflection of the glass. His voice was thick when he spoke. "It's the elderly man in the tan jacket. Your five o'clock."

She angled herself so the shop window reflected the street behind her. It took her a few seconds to spot him. His height, build and dress were nearly indistinguishable from the other merchants and workers in the market, but Adelaide supposed that was the point. Barrow's words in the Conciergerie echoed in her mind. *You have to look the part to play the part.* "Was the clover upside down or right-side up?"

Teo pulled his eyes from the dress and met hers in the polished window. "Upside down"

"Good, that means it's safe to talk to him."

The man purchased something from the stand. The merchant passed back a couple of bills, which the man stuffed in his pockets, along with his hands, and headed to the edge of the market.

"Let's go," Adelaide folded herself into the crowd behind the man.

The two of them followed him deeper into the city. Though the streets weren't quite as labyrinthine as the ones in France, they still held their fair share of twists and turns, dark alleys and dilapidated buildings. For a city, it had a more of a small town feel and, with what Adelaide knew about Richmond in the 1860s, it operated like one too. If anyone watched them for too long, they would know they were outsiders.

The man ducked down a side street and into a storefront. Adelaide and Teo paused at the corner, waiting a few beats before they approached it. Faded letters on the door told her it was another tailor shop, this one a shadow of the one in the market. Paint flaked on the siding, and a yellow haze tinged the glass in the windows. Adelaide pulled open the door and entered the shop, the floor creaking beneath her weight as Teo followed a few steps behind.

Thick air enveloped the inside in a stifling heat that quickly coated her brow in a thin sheen of sweat. She dragged a sleeve across her forehead, wishing for a few less layers of fabric and lace to make the heat a little more bearable. Shelves, piled high with fabrics of every color, towered above them. Mannequins pinned up in half-finished outfits stood haphazardly arranged around a four-foot platform, a bolt of strawberry-colored fabric sprawled across its surface. Every inch of wall not hidden by a shelf was covered in pants and dresses, jackets and Confederate uniforms, all suspended from hooks like ornaments on a Christmas tree.

A soft click like the turn of a lock emitted behind her, and before Adelaide could face the noise, she felt the barrel of a gun settle between her shoulder blades. She stilled, memories of the guards in the Conciergerie flashing through her mind as her eyes met Teo's at the back of the room.

"Are ya'll gonna tell me why you've been followin' me?" a gravelly voice grunted. "Or should I shoot now and tell the papers it was a robbery gone wrong?"

"I doubt they would believe that." Teo's hand moved slowly to his hip. "Doesn't seem like there's anything here worth stealing."

Adelaide bristled. Was he trying to get her killed?

Teo slipped his hand inside his jacket, but before he could grip his gun, the man dug the barrel harder into Adelaide's back. She stumbled forward. "Ah, ah, ah. Don't think about going for your piece. I can pull this trigger faster than ya can grab it."

Adelaide could see Teo weighing his options. After a second that felt like eternity, he dropped his hands and spread them wide. "Take it easy."

"What do you want?"

"Elizabeth Van Lew." The words tumbled out of her mouth before Adelaide had the chance to think about whether they were the right ones to say.

Teo shot her a look, but she didn't care. He wasn't the one on the wrong end of a gun.

"What do you want with Elizabeth?"

"We just want to talk."

"It's okay, John," a woman's voice said behind her. "Let's hear them out."

Adelaide felt the pressure of the gun ease off her skin and dared a slow turn to face the man and the woman who'd joined him. She blended with the shadows cast across the room, and the folds of her simple gown were like wisps of smoke from a dying flame. She had dull hair and an unremarkable face, with sharp angles like a Picasso. Not quite ugly or pretty, but perfectly plain in a way that would fade from memory if you glanced away for too long. Easily forgotten.

"We heard you're building up a network of spies to help the Union win the war," Adelaide said, putting together who the woman was. "We want to help."

Elizabeth watched her, sizing Adelaide up. Her face gave nothing away, remaining unchanged, save for the slight arc of a single brow. "Where are you from?"

Adelaide fumbled, thrown off guard by the shift in conversation. "Ah, New York, originally." She thought back to the folder Dr. Jameson had given her, trying to remember her persona's backstory. "My husband and I moved to Virginia a year ago to settle his late-father's estate. Before we got around to moving back, the country was at war."

"And where's your husband now?" Elizabeth said, clasping her hands in front of her.

"Dead. At Sumter."

Elizabeth nodded, though Adelaide couldn't tell if she believed the lie or not. "My condolences."

"Thank you."

"So you want revenge on those who killed your loved one. Is that it?" Elizabeth said, starting to move about the room.

Her questions made Adelaide feel like she had whiplash. One after the other they hit her in succession the moment after she thought she had finally found her footing again. Elizabeth was testing her, and Adelaide knew it. There was a reason she had been able to do what she did. Elizabeth was smart and calculating. She wasn't going to admit to starting up an espionage ring to a stranger, let alone trust them without reason.

Adelaide chose her words carefully, hoping they were the right ones. "I'd be lying if I said I didn't want revenge. Loss is a wound that never truly heals. But more than that, I want the slaves freed and the war ended before another man's blood runs red in the fields."

Elizabeth stopped walking and leaned back against a shelf with her gaze fixed on Adelaide. "That, my dear, is something we have in common. But I'm afraid I cannot help you."

"But—"

"Put the gun down, John." Elizabeth turned and pulled a dress down from the wall.

John slowly lowered the gun, though he didn't look all that happy about it.

"I'll be back at the usual time." Elizabeth handed John a bill before heading to the door. She hesitated at the threshold and looked back over her shoulder at Adelaide. "If what you said about your desire to help was true, there are many ways to win a war. They might not let us fight on the battlefield, but we can still fight, nonetheless. Figure out what you will be proud to have done when the war is over and do it the best way you know how. Even if someone tells you no."

"Where the hell were you?" Teo all but shouted at Mikaelson as they neared him and the invisible time machine.

Mikaelson sat on a log nearby, a pile of shavings at his feet. More fell to ground as he ran his knife skillfully down the length of a piece of wood, whittling. "I had some rather unexpected business to attend to."

"And you couldn't have told us that before leaving us in the middle of 1860s Richmond?" Adelaide asked, hiking up her skirts.

"I could have," Mikaelson stood. He threw his stick hard to the ground, and its newly sharpened end sank into the earth. "But there wasn't time. I like you kids. I really do, but I've been working a mission here for far too long and have lost far too much to have the two of you screw it up."

Adelaide remembered the time machine on the day they were supposed to jump for the first time. Kolt had said it was broken from a recent mission. Had Mikaelson been a part of it?

"What do you mean?" Adelaide asked.

Mikaelson sighed, a weary look in his eye. "What we do shouldn't be possible and even though we can go back doesn't always mean we should. History isn't kind, and although it's already been written, reliving it never quite goes how you expect it to. People get hurt, people die and you can't fix it. Even when you have a time machine." He shook his head. "Anyway, we should get going. Our time is almost up, and I need to get out of this uniform. How'd it go with Van Lew?"

"It didn't," Adelaide said.

"Well," Mikaelson punched the keys on the time machine, turning it visible. "I'll let you be the one to tell Jameson that. Let's go."

13

WORDS FROM THE PAST

———

Afternoon sunlight filtered through the rose window and danced flecks like rainbow jewels across the pages as Adelaide read. Juniper had left for a meeting, but not before piling Adelaide's arms high with leather-bound volumes on the Civil War and Mary Stuart.

She found her way to a desk on the topmost floor of the library. It sat near the central railing that followed the curve of the stained-glass dome above. The floor stretched out in all directions with bookshelves scattered around haphazardly like the paths of a labyrinth, offering pockets of seclusion. The only eyes watching were chiseled in marble and belonged to the statues on pedestals rimming the space beneath the dome.

Though her eyes were between the pages, Adelaide's mind was somewhere else, swirling about like a whirlpool. She was just starting the same paragraph for the third time when a shadow fell over her. She looked up as Kolt pulled out the chair across from her and flipped it. He sat, his legs on either side of the back, and folded his arms over the top. A stray strand of dark hair, stark against his olive skin and emerald eyes, fell across his forehead as he leaned toward her. "I must say, Adelaide, of all the places around here you could have been, I am utterly shocked to have found you in the library with your nose in a book."

"Really?" Adelaide marked her spot with her thumb. "Where did you think I'd be?"

A smile teased his lips. "My bet was in the gym for boxing lessons."

"Well, I hope you didn't wager anything too important."

Kolt shrugged. "Just a kidney. Good thing I'm not too attached to it." He squinted at the book in her hands. "What are you reading?"

She held it up so he could see the title. "It's about Mary Stuart. I figured since she is my ancestor, it wouldn't hurt to learn a bit more about her. I was hoping it might help me understand her a little better."

Kolt laughed, the motion deepening the dimple in his cheek. The sound, though a little too loud for a library, was thick and fruity like the pop of champagne bubbles.

"What's so funny?

Kolt gently pulled the book from her hands and set it on the table. "Forget the books, Ad. You're in Scotland. That," he said, motioning toward the book, "is no way to learn about Mary." He jumped to his feet and extended a hand to her.

"If you really want to get in her head, you have to walk in her footsteps."

"Here, put this on," Kolt said, handing Adelaide a helmet.

They stood on the worn path at the base of the ruins. Damp earth perfumed the air in soil and musk stirred by the gentle breeze off the loch. Adelaide pushed the curls from her face and breathed in the sweet air of the green hillside. She hadn't realized how much she had missed the freedom of the outdoors. Though she had only been in headquarters for a few days, the feel of a natural landscape beneath her feet was a welcomed relief from the stone walls and dark corridors of the castle.

The old Adelaide would have thought twice before hopping on the back of a boy's bike, even if that boy was a long-lost childhood friend. But if the last few days had taught her anything, it was that she couldn't go back to being the girl she was before. She'd fallen too far down the rabbit hole to climb back out now. She took the helmet and put it on. "Where are we going?"

Kolt kicked up the stand and mounted his bike. "Wherever you want. We just have one stop we need to make first, though."

Adelaide hopped on behind him and wrapped her arms around his waist.

Kolt peered over his shoulder, eying her through the shield of his helmet. "All set?"

"Yeah," Adelaide said, thankful her own helmet hid the blush she could feel heating her cheeks.

Kolt revved the engine, the bike humming to life beneath them, and kicked off the ground. Adelaide gripped him tighter as the world flew by in a blur of color like the shifting gems of a kaleidoscope. Every mile of road that passed beneath their tires took a worry with it until Adelaide found herself feeling completely and utterly free. "Faster," she shouted in the wind. Though she couldn't hear it, she felt Kolt laugh as he pushed the throttle and the bike gained speed.

Country hills slowly faded into city streets, and all too soon they were slowing back down. Buildings with antique façades stacked together like dominos on either side of the ancient street. People wove in and out of the light traffic chatting as they ran errands and walked through the shops dotting the avenue. Kolt veered down a side street and worked his way to a small parking lot at the back of a two-story brick building. They hopped off and rounded the corner of the building to a chipped door set into the wall that read *The Bean of Scots*. Kolt held the door for her. His shoulders relaxed as they stepped inside.

The sharp blend of coffee grounds and sugar greeted them as their eyes adjusted to the dim light. The same exposed brick on the outside continued within the structure. Edison bulbs flickered overhead in staggered groups of three like mobiles, their light casting a honey-golden glow over the room. Low tables filled an indent in the right wall, mirrored on the left by a countertop piled high with glass-cased pastries. Adelaide scouted a table while Kolt ordered. He found her moments later and worked his way to the table, his limp more noticeable than normal on the uneven floor. He set a steaming cup of cream-colored liquid in front of her and sat down. Adelaide curled her fingers around the cup and welcomed its warmth.

"Thanks," she raised the mug to her lips and took a sip. "Woah," Adelaide said, surprised by the medley of flavors that hit her tongue in a perfect blend of sweet cream, dark chocolate and cinnamon. "What is this?"

"No idea," Kolt shrugged off his acid-wash denim jacket, slinging it over the back of his chair. "A local recommended it to me my first time here. I've been drinking it ever since."

"How'd you find this place, anyway?" They were miles from headquarters, off the main drag to Edinburgh. She'd recognized the road from her previous trip into the city with her mother years ago.

He took a sip from his mug and swiped the back of his hand over his lips. "Xander actually found it. He'd been looking for local haunts to sell some of his work a few years ago and brought me with when he made the sale to celebrate. I loved the place so much I rented the apartment above it. It was a bit of a mess, but between the two of us, we got it gutted and refurbished pretty quickly."

Adelaide could remember a time Xander followed Kolt like a shadow. As an only child, his elder cousin was the closest thing Xander had to a brother. Even when Kolt's family had moved away, the two remained nearly inseparable. But in the time she had reconnected with both Kolt and Xander, it had become clear to her that something had changed that. "Does he visit often? It must be nice to have a place to get away to."

Kolt pushed his mug away and leaned back in his chair. "He did, for a while, when he wanted to paint in peace or he was fighting with my uncle. But not so much anymore."

"What happened?"

Kolt's eyes roamed the room, but whether he was actively looking for someone or trying to avoid her gaze, Adelaide couldn't tell. "That's a long story, and one better suited to another time if we want to get you back by sundown." After another glance, he dragged his eyes back to her. Their warmth and light reminded her of a jade-colored pool. "So tell me, where are we going?"

Adelaide wanted to know more, but she let the matter drop. In the time they had been sitting there, the day was already beginning to edge into the late afternoon hours. She thought of several places she wanted to go, but in the moment, she craved something familiar. "I was thinking maybe we could go to Holyrood Palace."

Before Kolt could respond, a man brushed by their table and slipped a manila file onto the wooden surface. Kolt stood and slid it off, tucking it to his side. He grabbed his jacket and slung it over his arm, concealing the file. Adelaide had expected him to say something about it, but he simply said, "Holyrood Palace it is. Just let me run this upstairs and we can get going."

For the second time in her life, Adelaide found herself on the grounds of Holyrood Palace. The castle rose before her as the afternoon sun cast a shadow across the drive. A mix of straight lines and curved turrets, the structure stretched out in all directions, a continuous rectangle of rooms wrapped around a plush, central courtyard. From a distance, the exterior appeared to be simple, but a closer view of the architectural work revealed an array of intricate care and detailing in the stone. As they neared the entrance, Adelaide half expected her mother to start spouting facts in the rapid-fire way she did when she was excited, her words tripping over one another, but the footsteps beside her belonged not to her mother but to Kolt.

Adelaide had asked Kolt about the file, but he simply brushed it off, saying it was for a personal project. He was a writer and sometimes the information he needed for bits of research were beyond his ability to retrieve, so he'd called in a favor. Adelaide wasn't sure what kind of writing required covert files from shady men in coffee shops off the beaten path, but she didn't question it too much. She had watched her own mother do a plethora of bizarre things in the name of research.

Adelaide recalled from her previous trip that Holyrood had become Mary's home upon the untimely death of her first husband, Francis. But as she wandered the halls, she was reminded once again of the depth of joy and pain they concealed. Mary's first and only child had been born here in her bedroom. Her friend and confidant, David Rizzio, murdered in the antechamber adjacent to that very spot, his blood still a faded red stain on the worn floorboards. For the first time Adelaide found herself wishing away the red ropes and glass cases meant to protect the past from wandering visitors. She wanted to run the length of the halls brushing her hands along anything she could and see what kind of stories would soak through her fingers from the floorboards. She wanted to feel the joy and pain, love and hatred that reminded her that the people in her books and traces weren't just figures in the past or characters in a story but flesh-and-blood people with failures and triumphs, hopes and heartbreaks.

They walked through several rooms and were now in Mary's antechamber, the room adjacent to her bedroom that she had used to receive guests and pray. Wooden beams crisscrossed the ceiling, segmenting it into a pattern like a monochromatic chessboard. Elaborate tapestries covered the walls in scenes from the Bible and Greek mythology, some even rumored to have been woven by Mary herself while in captivity. Whatever wall space was not occupied by a tapestry hosted a series of portraits depicting Scottish royals.

Adelaide walked past the plaque denoting the spot Rizzio was murdered to a glass case in the center of the room. A heart-shaped locket sat inside. Its surface was encrusted in rare gemstones. She read the nameplate, explaining that it was the Darnley Jewel, a family locket given to Mary by Henry Darnley upon the arrangement of their marriage in 1565.

"Time causes all to learn," Kolt said, coming up behind her.

"What?" Adelaide asked.

He shoved his hands in his pockets and nodded toward the locket. "It's a translation of one of the lines on the locket." He titled his head, his face wrought with thought as if he was mulling over the line like fine wine. "It's a nice thought. If only it were true. Though, I guess if it was, there'd be no need for us."

Though he didn't explicitly explain with strangers around, Adelaide gathered from the way he said it that "us" was the Red Rose Society. While she saw the value in what they were doing, what good was the ability to travel to the past and record it as it was if no one ever learned from it? Maybe that was what her traces were for—a way for history to show her what was so she could not just hope but actively pursue what could be. She thought about her most recent traces, the flash of crimson curls on a midnight ride and the girl in the wedding dress. Those ones, at least, seemed to have some cohesion to them. But the ones she'd had while in Revolutionary France didn't seem to connect at all, little girls in the Conciergerie, the man in the executioner's labyrinth, the faint and dreamlike memory of a woman in a tower. What if they weren't just mismatched pieces of the past but, instead, individual threads that needed to be woven together like the tapestries that lined the walls.

As the thought crossed her mind, a prick of discomfort settled behind her eyes, growing steadily greater. She closed them briefly and rubbed her forehead, trying to sort through the noise to distinguish the one calling loudest to her, but they blended to a painful white noise that made her teeth clench. She opened her eyes to Kolt's. An array of emotions crossed his face in a matter of moments and settled into a look she had seen far too many times in the mirror, raw and haunted. His mouth parted and shut with words unspoken. He cleared his throat. "Ah, are you done in here or was there more you wanted to see?"

It took a second for his words to clear the fog thickening in her head. "Uh, yeah. Let's go to the next room."

They were almost to the doorway when a shock of pain flared in her temple. Her breath hitched as she dropped her head and brought her fingers to the spot, sore and tender like a fresh bruise. She was vaguely aware of Kolt beside her, but his words blended into the white noise, and her attention fixed on an object in the glass case beside her. The plaque in front of it said it was a diary from one of Mary's ladies, yet, it's deep red-black leather brought her back not to the ancient past, but to a winter night fireside with her mother. She ached to reach beyond the red-velvet ropes, but even with the glass between it and her Adelaide knew she had found her mother's missing journal.

14

QUEEN'S BLOOD

Adelaide stepped outside, breathing in the sharp scent of fresh dew beginning to settle on the grass. She focused on the stars, each one like a splatter of diamonds across a dark velvet cloth, as she forced the cool night air in and out of her lungs in a steady rhythm. Her hands shook with adrenaline as the remnants of her smoke-filled dreams lingered.

The sun had nearly set, dipping the world in gold by the time she and Kolt arrived back at headquarters, but unlike the joy of the ride before, the trip back had lost its magic. Trees and street signs passed in a blur of grey as Adelaide lost herself in her head. Though she wasn't the only one. Kolt, too, remained silent. She had expected him to come inside and at least warm up for a bit. She had wanted the chance to explain her odd behavior today, at least the best she could, and give him a chance to explain his, but he had remained seated and wished her goodnight no sooner than her feet hit the packed earth. She could feel his eyes on her as she walked to the door. Only when it was firmly shut behind her did she hear the rev of his bike start and fade off into the night.

Adelaide walked to the edge of the loch, calmed by the gentle lap of water on shore. Ever since she was little, it was the one thing that continually helped to put her at ease. August rain on the roof. The rock of waves beneath Charlie's boat lulling her to sleep. The sinking of her feet in the sand on a wet beach, and the sharp bite of foam and chilled water as it circled her ankles. Even now, after the events of recent years, it remained a comforting presence. Though the sad poetry of it all wasn't lost on her—that water should be the thing she sought to quell the fires in her life.

Untying her high-tops, she tossed them up the slope and slipped her feet into the water. It was shallow where she stood, and the water level only rose a breadth past her ankles, but it was enough to clear her mind for a moment. Hours ago she had been so convinced the journal at Holyrood was her mother's, but the more she thought about it, the less sure she was. Every day that passed since the fire took a bit more of her parents with it. The details of their faces grew duller, the sound of their voices fainter. How long until time claimed every last remnant of them? How much of her memory could she actually trust when even the night of their deaths was shrouded in smoke?

She must have gotten the color wrong or the detailing in the leather. Had it been there the last time she was at Holyrood with her mother? Adelaide flipped through her memories, trying to dredge up the book from before, but the two of them had gone so many places in such little time that she couldn't distinguish if it had been there or not.

She set her gaze across the glassy surface of the loch and ran the charm of her necklace subconsciously between her fingers. Somewhere between the time her mother had given it to her the last time they were in Scotland together and the deaths of her parents, it had become her anchor, a grounding presence she found herself reaching for whenever the ground she stood on seemed to shift beneath her feet like quicksand. She still wasn't sure what had prompted the gift, and now that she knew about her connection to Mary Stuart, it seemed even more strange that the pendant would be a Tudor rose, a symbol more connected to Elizabeth than it was to Mary.

A dark object sat on the water and drew closer as it cut ripples through the glassy loch. It was a small boat, no bigger than the Viking-style canoes they had set aflame at Barrow and Jonas' funeral. She could just make out the outline of a lone figure seated inside. Only when it was a few yards off was she able to discern it was Teo. He wore all black, the tight form of a windbreaker molding to his figure. Though his face remained steady as the front of the boat bumped the shore beside her, his dark chocolate eyes glinted in the moonlight.

Adelaide was suddenly aware of how strange she must look, ankle deep in the loch in the late hours of the night. "Teo." She nodded at him, the pendant of her necklace still clasped between her fingers. "I'm sure you're wondering why I'm standing in the loch."

"Funny enough, the thought had crossed my mind." A smile teased the corners of his mouth, though it didn't quite reach his eyes. He ran a thumb beneath his bottom lip as if trying to smooth it out. "I'm sure you're wondering why I'm boating across it."

She let out a nervous laugh, echoing his words. "The thought had crossed my mind."

Teo jumped out of the boat onto shore and shoved it back out into the water. Moonlight lit the edges of him, dark threaded in silver. "Well then…" he extended a hand to her. She took it, allowing him to pull her out of the water beside him. She was close enough to smell his musk on the air they shared, feel the rough callus of his hand on her smooth palm. "Let's agree that if anyone asks, neither of us was here tonight."

Back inside headquarters, Adelaide had the sensation she was being watched. Though she was used to that feeling within headquarters, this time it was different. Footsteps behind her started and stopped as she did, quickened and slowed with her pace. Was she being followed? She paused, listening once again for the quick stutter step that stopped after her.

Doubling back, she crept lightly on the balls of her feet, hoping to catch a glimpse of her unwelcomed shadow. She turned the corner to where the footsteps had stopped, but the corridor was empty. She scanned the halls on either side for good measure, but whoever had been tailing her was long gone, concealed in a secret passageway or dark alcove. Adelaide knew from her own late-night wanderings around the halls that the castle had enough hidden places to get lost in.

Just in case, she took the corridor on her right. The darker of her three visible options, it seemed the most likely candidate for someone trying to disappear. She followed the dips and turns in the hall until it brightened, unexpectedly. Light seeped through a cracked door, splitting the darkness. Adelaide slowed, curious. Though she had been down this hall before, it had always been a series of oak doors, sealed tightly. Not even the few tricks Colden had taught her about picking locks had worked on them. She crept closer, her weight against the thin strip of wall beside the hinges.

Through the crack in the door, she could see what looked like a sitting room. Two dark leather armchairs faced a large, arched window, framed on either side by heavy drapes. Stars pinpricked the inky night in a splatter of silver through the window. She leaned forward, hoping to catch a glimpse of whoever was inside, but her movement bumped the door, sending her across the threshold. Before she could flee, a man's voice on the other side called, "Hello?"

Caught, Adelaide moved the rest of the way in. She could now see that polished bookshelves ran the length of three walls, stretching nearly to the ceiling. The fourth housed a painting in a gilded frame that looked like a Degas, though it wasn't one she had ever seen before. A desk sat below it with the whorls of waves and sailing ships carved into the dark wood, and Gideon Hargrove stood behind it.

Her uncle looked tired. The slight waves in his greying, chestnut hair kinked at odd angles as if he had combed his fingers through it several times tonight. His weary eyes lightened with uncertainty and Adelaide could tell it had registered to him that the girl who had stumbled into his office was his estranged niece. "Hey, kid."

"*Adelaide* is fine." She hadn't planned for her words to sound so harsh, but truth be told she still wasn't sure how she felt about her uncle. Half of her was angry, and rightfully so. He had all but disappeared from her life for nearly half of it. But the other half belonged to a girl who couldn't help but want to cling to the only piece of family she had left.

He winced, smoothing his hands down the front of his wrinkled shirt. "Right, *Adelaide*. Please, have a seat. Would you like a cup of tea?"

Without waiting for her reply, Gideon walked to a bar cart beside the window. Instead of scotch and gin, it held an assortment of tea and sugar cubes, two of which he was placing in the bottom of a chipped mug. Adelaide sat in a leather chair and watched him pour hot water from a brass kettle over the sugar. Time had touched the man that for so long had seemed untouchable. Though, despite the years, his features still held a refined, handsome charm that her mother had said used to get him into a healthy dose of trouble.

"Rose tea, from my latest trip to England." He stood before her, mug in hand. "And two sugar cubes." He smiled, proud to remember her tea preference. She didn't have the heart to tell him that in the time he missed, her taste had changed. Gideon extended the mug to her like an olive branch.

She slowly extended her own hand and took it. "Thank you."

Gideon eased into the chair opposite her. Adelaide sipped her tea, steam heating her face as she wondered, among other things, why rose tea and sugar cubes was a drink she had relegated to the sick days and tea parties of her childhood. Silence stretched between them, emphasized by a syncopated rhythm that was either the ticking of a grandfather clock or the pulsing of Adelaide's heartbeat in her ears. She searched her mind and the room for a place to start. On the table between them sat a chess board, checkered squares of alabaster and red patterning its surface. Marble figurines in corresponding colors sat atop, poised mid-game.

"You play chess?"

"Ah, yes." Gideon reached up, rubbing the tension from his neck with a tanned hand. "Actually, your mother taught me. Bought me the board, too."

He watched her. Adelaide could tell he was testing the water, but she wasn't quite ready to dive in too deep just yet. "And your opponent just walked out on you?"

"Not exactly," he picked up a red king and moved it forward on the board. "I was playing myself. It helps me clear my mind when I need to think."

Adelaide leaned forward and moved the white queen.

He raised an eyebrow, impressed by the speed and skill of her move. "I see Anna taught you a thing or two as well. Care to finish the game with some stakes? That is, if you haven't outgrown that competitive streak of yours."

Adelaide tilted her head, sizing him up. She could never resist a challenge. "What exactly did you have in mind?"

"I know we both have questions, and I'm sure we're both hoping for some answers." Gideon countered her move with a knight. "So, I propose we play, whenever you want, with two simple rules: winner asks a question, and loser answers truthfully."

Adelaide moved her queen again, checking his king in a manner impossible to break. "Where have you been all these years?"

Weariness settled over Gideon's features. "You are your mother's daughter, never afraid to ask questions, especially ones with complex answers." he sighed, setting his mug atop the faded ring of a watermark on the coffee table. "Very well. Truth be told, it would be easier to answer with the places I haven't been. I've seen more of this world in the past decade than many see in a lifetime."

Adelaide had expected that to be the end of his answer, but he continued, regaling her with stories of dives along the Great Barrier Reef, treks through the Amazon Rainforest and spelunking in the Cave of Crystals. Each tale was as spectacular as the last, and Adelaide could feel the tension within her ease into the comfortability of his skill. She had forgotten what it had been like to listen to her mother and uncle tell stories in a way that seemed as natural as breathing. She wanted to stay in the warmth of his study and soak in everything he had to say, but even as she lost herself in the world of his words, another question pushed past her lips.

"Why?" she breathed, cutting off yet another daring tale.

Gideon's smile faltered.

Though she couldn't keep the question at bay, Adelaide didn't expect him to give her an answer. At least not until another match secured her an additional victory.

Gideon stood and walked, once again, to the bar cart. Stooping, he opened a small set of double doors at the base and pulled out a decanter. He poured the amber liquid into the bottom of a crystal glass and tipped it back. Returning to his seat, he met her gaze as a flush heated his cheeks. "What do you know about time travel? About the mechanics of what makes it possible?"

She didn't see how his question related to her own, but whatever information he was about to share, she certainly wasn't going to stop him. "Nothing. Up until a few weeks ago, I didn't even know it was possible."

Gideon's thumb worried at a brass button on his chair. "Well, it is. Largely because of this." He reached into his pocket and set the contents on the coffee table between them.

She picked it up, holding it to the light for a better view. It was a small stone, no bigger than a golf ball. It reminded her of the uncut rubies her father would sometimes find on a dig.

The raw stone was similar in color but a darker shade of red. Up close, she could also see veins of onyx shot through the gem. "What is it?"

Gideon leaned toward her. "It's a gemstone known by many names to those of us who are aware of its existence, but its most commonly called *reginae sanguine*."

Adelaide turned the Latin phrase over in her mind, translating it. "Queen's Blood."

Gideon nodded, extending his hand for the stone, and she placed it in his palm. This time, he held it to the light. "Legend says that whenever a queen's blood is spilled and mixes with the Earth, a stone is formed. In large enough quantities, its properties power the time machine. Add in some coding to pinpoint a location and additional electricity to heat the gemstone and, well, you know the rest."

"So the gemstone powers the time machine, but how does that explain why you left?"

Gideon glanced at the bar cart and ran a hand across his brow. "I will tell you. God knows I owe you more than words, but you have to agree that what I say next remains between us. For your own safety as well as mine, no one can know I shared this with you."

"Okay." Adelaide locked her eyes with his. "I promise."

He held her gaze. "Queen's Blood is a rare gemstone to begin with, but it's become increasingly hard to find. The Red Rose

Society's store of it has been depleting for years. If they don't acquire more soon, time travel will cease to exist within the next few years. Possibly sooner."

Adelaide finally understood how everything he had said connected with her question. "They sent you to find more."

15

FRACTURED PAST

———

Adelaide stared up at the colored dome overhead. She was back in the library, lying on a table in the same spot Kolt had found her the day he'd taken her to Holyrood. Keeping Elise company, she watched as the girl re-shelved a series of leather volumes.

Elise turned to her. "This can't be interesting to you. You're just avoiding having to meet Charlie for an afternoon of event planning for the gala. Aren't you?"

Though her eyes were on the painted ceiling, her mind was still on the night before, and she shrugged at Elise's query.

Of all the ways the first encounter with her uncle could have gone, Adelaide wouldn't have predicted it would include tea, chess, and an honest answer. Gideon had been true to his word, admitting far more than she had expected him to, including the fact that the Red Rose Society was running out of Queen's Blood to power the time machine. He hadn't left them because he wanted to but because he had to. No one could know what he was doing, and contact with anyone could have put his mission at risk. She knew his answer in no way made up for his absence, but at least she had finally gotten one.

She held her hand above her, watching light dance off the red rose on the ring she had received at initiation. Last night, Gideon had also told her that Queen's Blood was the same stone used for member rings. Since their conversation, Adelaide couldn't seem to get the gemstone out of her head. Other than the obvious, she couldn't figure out what about the stone had bugged her enough to burrow into her skin like a tick.

Adelaide tilted her hand, revealing the thick scarring on her palm. As she gazed at the still-healing skin, an image of the earring, glistening red in her hand, flashed across her mind. She shot upright on the table. The earring. It had been set in the very same stone.

"Ready to drop these off in archives?" Elise asked, snapping Adelaide out of her reverie and handing her a stack of books.

Adelaide tried not to recoil as she took them and felt grateful the press of her skin against the books didn't spark a trace. "Yeah, lead the way."

She followed Elise back down to the main floor of the library to a door on the far-side wall. Elise slipped a metal skeleton key into the lock and shouldered open the door, revealing a dimly lit room. "Room" was too loose a term for the space, which resembled something closer to a warehouse. Books and artifacts of all kinds lay scattered about on a mix of metal and wooden shelves, but there was a sense of organization to the chaos that told her everything was exactly where it was supposed to be. Every object had a tag attached to it. The black ink of feminine script denoted what it was and the corresponding year it belonged to. Adelaide wasn't entirely sure what all being a Keeper entailed, but if the threat of sparking a trace wasn't looming over her head, she would have loved to learn.

"Where do these go?" Adelaide asked, feeling the beginnings of a headache prick at her temples. She wanted to get them put away and get out of the room, hoping to avoid having a trace in front of Elise. She trusted the girl a lot more than she did many others within the Red Rose Society, but still, the fewer people who knew her secret, the better.

Elise scanned the stack, checking the spines. She closed her eyes, tongue clenched between her teeth in concentration. Her eyes remained shut as she gestured around the room, using her eidetic memory to recall each volume's correct location. "The top two go in Beethoven's piano bench, the red one in the pocket of Amelia Earhart's flying jacket and the last one in the armoire from the *Titanic*." She opened her eyes, a wry smile on her face. "That one's in the back, by the way, right past the missing half of the Sphinx's nose."

"Got it," Adelaide called over her shoulder as she headed deeper into the shelves.

She returned all the books to their proper locations and was headed back to where she had left Elise when the pain in her head intensified, hot and sharp like an iron prod. Adelaide gasped and doubled over, gripping the shelf beside her so tightly the metal bit into her palm. She closed her eyes against the pain and let it lead her like a magnet through the archives. After several minutes, Adelaide felt herself slow to a stop. She opened her eyes to find she was crouched in front of a black vintage suitcase. As she eased it open, she half-expected the case to be the thing that was calling to her, but instead, her eyes and fingertips met with a leather-bound ledger.

As her fingers grazed its surface, the book fell open and images started to take form. Adelaide watched as a woman, her face indistinguishable, dipped a fountain pen into an inkwell and proceeded to dance the pen across the worn page in looping swirls. A symbol like the inverted blade of a guillotine glistened in gold ink on her wrist and Adelaide recognized it as the marking of a Keeper. The same one Juniper had. After a final stroke, the woman set the pen down. Adelaide could now see the words, glistening in the candlelight as they dried: *Sienna Baird*.

"Ad," Elise called.

Adelaide startled, dropping the ledger. Disconnected from her touch, the images faded before she could discern anything else. She moved to retrieve it, but stopped short as her gaze fell on the open page, the same one she'd watched the woman write on. It held a list of names. Her eyes scanned it for the girl's, but in the location it should have been, the page was empty. The only markings there were the faded ink lines of an *S* and a *B* in a row together. Elise called for her again. Adelaide quickly covered her fingers with her sleeve and picked up the ledger, slipping it in the waistband of her jeans, between the thin fabric of her t-shirt and the knitting of her cardigan. "I'm coming,"

Adelaide and Elise were halfway out of the library when Juniper's voice called out behind them. Adelaide bristled, slipping an arm behind her as she turned to face the woman. She could feel the ledger, hot against the small of her back, through her shirt. Had Juniper seen her take it?

"Hey, sugar, didn't know you were here," Juniper said with warmth in her violet eyes. "Helping Elise restock?"

"Yeah," Adelaide said, rubbing the back of her neck with her other hand. "Figured she could use the company."

Juniper smiled. "That was nice of you." She turned to Elise. "Elise, dear, would you mind holding down my office for the next hour? I'm afraid I have to duck out for a bit."

"Not at all," Elise said.

Juniper handed over her keys to Elise and hurried out of the library.

Adelaide let out a breath, a little shakier than she had intended, and let her hand drop to her side.

A loud crack, like the Earth splitting in two, suddenly shook the library. Adelaide staggered on her feet, nearly sent to the ground by the intense movement. Time seemed to slow as her fingers curled around the polished wood of a support column and her eyes focused on the ceiling. She watched as a gash, like the jagged edge of a lightning bolt, fissured across the dome overhead. A series of smaller cracks webbed from it across the surface of the frescoes, sending a piece of painted plaster the size of a manhole cover to the floor. Adelaide threw herself to the ground and covered her head as the piece shattered on impact. Dust and debris hit her skin and stuck to the sweat coating her arms.

"Ad, what's wrong?" Elise said, a panic in her voice.

Hands shook her, and she opened her eyes to find Elise standing over her with concern etched on her face. Adelaide panted and flicked her eyes from the ground to her arms and up to the dome, completely intact. "I'm okay, I must have passed out or something." *Or something*, she thought as she let Elise pull her to her feet.

"Are you sure you're all right?" Elise didn't seem convinced.

"I'm fine," Adelaide said, though she felt far from it.

Elise eyed her, a beat passing before she spoke again. "No, you're not." She grabbed Adelaide's wrist and pulled her into the stacks. "You've been acting weird since we got back from France. What is it?"

Adelaide thought about lying, but she knew she couldn't hide the truth from Elise forever. They were roommates, and at this point, maybe even friends. As a Keeper in training, she might even be able to help. At some point, Adelaide knew she had to start trusting someone. Once the words pushed past her lips, they flowed freely until she had told Elise nearly all of it; about the night of the fire, the gaps in her memory, the suspicions she had and the traces she'd seen. Elise remained quiet, her usually readable face a mask.

Adelaide finished, waiting for Elise's response. She expected her to say something, but instead, Elise punched her in the arm.

"Ow." Adelaide rubbed the spot Elise had hit. "What was that for?"

"That," Elise said, folding her arms across her chest, "is for waiting so long to tell me. I'll check the archives and see if I can find anything. If there's a mention of anything close to your traces, I'll find it."

"Thank you," Adelaide said, feeling slightly lighter now that she had finally shared her secret. "Can I ask you a question?"

Elise nodded. "Shoot,"

"The frescoes," Adelaide flicked her eyes to the dome, now in the distance. "Do you know what's painted on them?"

"Juniper said they're inflection points of the past, central moments on the timeline that, if altered, would wreck time as we know it. I'm still learning, but that's part of what Juniper does as a Keeper. She discovers, records and tracks the inflection points. And when a Timewalker comes back, she makes sure those points haven't changed."

Adelaide recalled the fissure on the dome's surface and the shatter of plaster on the ground. Juniper's words from the other day flitted across her mind, *all those things we didn't believe possible, might just be. Because of you.*

16

FEATHER AND INK

Adelaide walked into the room where the auction would be held. Intricate windows, interlaced with metal framework, spanned the length of an entire wall, flooding the room in midday light. It danced off the crystal chandeliers overhead, sending flecks of tiny rainbows around the room. The rest of the space was dark wood and bright gold, which shone like sunrays when the light glanced off the gilded surface. Though a fresh coat of polish covered the worn floorboards, she could almost hear the scrape of shoes wearing grooves into the wood from years of noblemen twirling women of prestige around the dance floor in a flurry of colored skirts.

She scanned the ballroom for Charlie's champagne curls, but they weren't yet among the few people gathered to help set up for the event. Adelaide recognized a few faces from the gala, but none enough to recall a name or approach them. Everyone bustled about, arranging elaborate bouquets and hanging banners that sported the name and logo of Harvard's Center for Marine Biology. A woman on a makeshift stage tested the microphone as a few other volunteers placed the last few chairs in the rows that faced it.

Colden sat in the last row. He leaned back in his chair, one foot propped on his knee as he flipped the pages of a newspaper. Adelaide rounded the end of the aisle and plopped down in the seat beside him. "This seat taken?"

"Anson, just the woman I need," Colden said, the blunt end of a pencil gripped between his teeth in thought. "What's a five-letter word for *stealthy kleptomaniac*?"

"*Thief*," Adelaide responded, after some thought.

Colden chuckled to himself as he penciled *thief* in the boxes for five across. "Bet the crossword team got a kick out of that one after last night."

Adelaide quirked her head, propping her arm on the back of her seat as she turned toward him. "What do you mean?"

Colden shifted the paper so she could see the front page. Adelaide was just starting to comprehend the headline when he said, "Holyrood was broken into last night."

Adelaide's heart squeezed with tension as she gripped the paper and scanned the article. "What did they take?"

Colden shook his head, his eyebrows scrunched in perplexation. "That's the thing. Security did a full sweep when the breech was discovered. Nothing's missing. Guess the thief got scared off before he could nab anything."

"Guess so..." Adelaide knew the history of Holyrood wasn't the only rich part of the estate. Between the portraits on the walls and jewels throughout the rooms, enough items of value would fetch millions on the black market with the right buyer. If they had already broken in, it would have taken mere seconds to smash a glass case and pocket the item inside. What kind of thief breaks in but doesn't steal? "Do they know who did it?"

"Not a clue," Colden folded the paper and set it on the seat beside him. "The article says the investigation is still underway, but it doesn't sound like they're hopeful they'll find anything. Whoever it was knew what they were doing."

Colden proceeded to regale her with tales of his favorite museum heists, gesturing dramatically as he wove the stories together in what Adelaide could only assume was a colorful way. On a normal day, she would have listened intently, even added in her own theories and speculations of those and other historical mysteries, but Adelaide, stuck with the odd feeling that tied her stomach in knots, tuned him out.

She suddenly realized Colden was asking her a question, but Charlie's voice from behind saved her from answering. "I always suspected it was the mob, but Ad has her own theories on the Gardner Heist." Charlie braced her hands on the back of Adelaide's chair and leaned forward with a teasing smile on her lips. "But you'll have to block off a few hours on your calendar to hear it since her stories tend to run down a hundred different rabbit trails before she gets to the point."

Adelaide smacked Charlie with the newspaper and laughed. "Do not."

"You do too, and you know it." Charlie reached over the back of Adelaide's chair and wrapped her in a playful hug. "But that's why we love you."

Pulling away, Charlie turned to Colden and flashed a million-dollar smile Adelaide knew she only broke out for special occasions. "Did you bring the painting? I can't wait to see it. I already know of three potential buyers eager to bid on it."

Colden rose slowly to his feet, gripping the front of his jacket with pride. "Of course. Let me show you."

They moved out of the aisle. Colden extended his arm to Charlie with an elegant bow straight from an Austen novel. "My lady."

Charlie took his arm and threw Adelaide a wink over her shoulder. Colden beckoned her along. As he led them across the room, he told them both more about the artist he was representing, taking care to mention the desire both he and the artist had to help contribute to such a worthy cause. Pierre Le Fleur was apparently well-known in his prime and had decided to make a re-entrance into the art world in a modern style completely unlike his previous works. The piece he had donated was the first in a new series he was unveiling next month in Italy.

Colden's eyes lit with passion as he spoke, reminding Adelaide of the way Xander's eyes would do the same whenever he had an idea for a new piece. He'd run into their clubhouse, words tumbling from his mouth as his hand began sketching concepts on the walls. She thought of the lighthouse he was working on now with the dark waves and sprays of foam breaking against the rocks. It was a far cry from the silver knights and golden dragons of his youth.

In the corner of the room, beside the makeshift stage, a series of tables were set up, overflowing with a variety of old and new items alike. Colden pulled a pair of white gloves from his pocket and slipped them over his fingers before gently picking up a painting that had been propped against the wall. He pulled the sheet off, slow and teasing, building anticipation to his final reveal of the artwork. It was a modern piece consisting of bold colors and black lines intersecting in a way Adelaide was sure made sense to the artist, but she could not for the life of her make out what it was supposed to be. It wasn't the kind of art she ever found herself drawn to, but it was exactly the kind people with wealth liked to hang on the walls of their penthouse suites.

After several words of approval from Charlie, Colden covered the painting back up and returned it to its spot against the wall. With a final wave to Adelaide and glance back at Charlie, he headed off to find Matriarch and finalize the donation. Charlie clapped her hands together in excitement as she got down to business. Their job was to catalog auction items and tag them each with the proper information. Adelaide eyed the items as a dull ache settled behind her eyes. Hoping he hadn't gotten too far yet, she whipped around and called Colden's name. Thankfully he was only a few yards away, roped into a conversation with a woman Adelaide didn't recognize.

Colden excused himself from the conversation and made his way back to them. "What's up?"

"Do you mind if I borrow your gloves?" Adelaide pushed a stray curl aside. She hoped she didn't look as desperate as she felt. "You can never be too careful when you're handling antiques."

"Sure," Colden removed the gloves from inside his jacket pocket and handed them to her. "Keep them. I've got enough pairs for the hands of half the mimes in Paris."

Adelaide thanked him and slipped the gloves on as he walked away. How much longer could she keep her secret hidden? If Colden hadn't been there with an extra pair of gloves, how many antiques passing through her hands would it have taken to spark a trace? It was nearly impossible to avoid touching something with history in headquarters. The building itself, though rebuilt and updated in several places, still contained pieces of the ancient structure. It was only a matter of time before someone witnessed a *trace*. She had to figure out what they meant and how to control them before she had one in front of the wrong person. Hopefully Elise would turn up something in her search.

A few hours later Adelaide and Charlie finished tagging the final donations. She had been worried at first that even with the gloves on a *trace* would still occur, but the afternoon passed without incident. Adelaide pulled the gloves from her fingers and stuck them in her back pocket as Charlie threw herself into the nearest chair with a sigh. "Remind me why I volunteered for this."

Adelaide crossed her arms and leaned back against the table. "Because you like event planning and you're a sucker for marine life."

"Right, I knew there was a good reason." Charlie glanced around the room. "Well, it looks like everything is nearly done. Wanna grab a bite to eat? We haven't exactly gotten to talk much since you showed up. Want to hit the town for a good old-fashioned girls' night, my treat?"

"Well, if you're buying, how can I refuse?"

"Sorry, ladies."

Adelaide turned to see Matriarch approaching, the click of her heels announcing her presence. Unlike that night in the corridor, her hair was back in its usual coil at the base of her neck. "Your girls' night is going to have to wait a few minutes more. I just had another donor drop this off, and I need it inventoried with the rest of the items."

Before Adelaide could react, Matriarch placed the objects in her hands. She gasped. In the second it took Adelaide to register the inkwell and feather pen in her palm, a pain flared in her head as a *trace* unfolded before her.

A man sat at a desk in a dark room. Though he was draped in furs, he shivered, his breath frozen in the air as he dipped his feather pen in the inkwell. He proceeded to scrawl hasty lines across the surface of the unbound vellum pages before him. Flames from the taper candles around him flickered out one by one. The sillage of their smoke trails wafted in the air like a charmed snake. As the flames died out, his fervor persisted, stopping only to replace the diminished candles with fresh ones. Young flames sprang to life, lighting the man's features. Though his hair was longer and the scruff on his face several days past a five-o'clock shadow, Adelaide recognized his eyes. They were kind and cold, youthful and ancient. An unchanged contradiction on the face of a man Adelaide had last seen several centuries ago in a graveyard. As he leaned forward to retrieve a fresh page, a gold pendant slipped from beneath the fold of his shirt.

The world slid back into view as the scene faded, a buzzing still ringing in Adelaide's ears. Charlie stood in front of her with a face etched in worry. "Are you okay?"

She really wished people would stop asking her that.

Matriarch eased her back onto a chair she had swiped from the front row.

"Yeah," Adelaide said, quickly slipping the feather pen and inkwell onto the table behind her. "I'm just a little light headed. Probably because I haven't eaten anything today."

"Don't get up just yet." Charlie said. "Let me get these cataloged, and then we can go and get you some food."

Charlie grabbed her clipboard and proceeded to log the items.

Matriarch remained beside her. She leaned in, her breath hot on Adelaide's neck as she whispered in her ear. "See anything interesting?"

17

A HANKERING FOR CRANACHAN

Adelaide sat outside on a small patio with Charlie. Strings of lights draped above them, blending with the night so each bulb flickered like fireflies in the city against the dark sky. Edinburgh was beautiful at night. It reminded Adelaide of a fairytale city that came to life with a timeless magic as soon as the sun slipped beneath the horizon. A full moon hung overhead, casting the dark silhouettes of the ancient architecture in a silver sheen like a coating of pixie dust.

"What did I tell you," Charlie said as Adelaide took a bite of her dessert. "This place has the best cranachan in Scotland."

Though it was the only cranachan she had ever tried, Adelaide had to agree it was quite impressive. The sharp bite of fresh raspberry and smooth cream blended like a symphony on her tongue. She was glad Charlie had suggested they go out for the night. If Adelaide tried hard enough, she could almost convince herself that things were normal, almost like they had been before. Before the fire. Before the Red Rose Society. Before time travel, secrets, and unanswered questions. But the bliss of pretending only ever lasted so long.

Adelaide rubbed a finger absentmindedly through the condensation on her wine glass. Charlie's smile dipped, sensing the change in her mood before Adelaide had even realized it herself. She signaled for the bill and threw a wad of cash on the table. Shivering despite the warmth in the summer breeze that lifted her curls, Adelaide shrugged on her jacket. They left the restaurant and followed the streets through the heart of the city. Though Adelaide hadn't said a word, Charlie knew the question poised on her lips would come out eventually. "Go ahead. Ask it."

Adelaide shoved her hands in her pockets and pursed her lips, unsure if she was ready for the answer. "Why didn't you tell me about all of this?"

"Haven't you learned by now that it's not something you tell." Charlie slid her eyes around the street as if looking for figures that weren't there. Her voice dropped, not quite to a whisper, but low enough that her words would be lost in the wind if Adelaide wasn't walking right beside her. "It's something you hide."

"That was at least better than Xander's answer." Adelaide pulled a scrunchie from her wrist, piling her hair into a messy bun atop her head. "He said it was to protect me."

Charlie tilted her head, brushing a hand through her waves. "In a way, it was. The Red Rose Society has its own set of rules. I don't envy anyone who breaks them."

Adelaide thought about Kolt and the warning he had given her when she'd first arrived and hadn't recognized him, the slight hitch in his step just awkward enough to be noticeable. "Is that what happened to Kolt?"

"Honestly, I'm not sure." Charlie bit her lip. "He doesn't talk about it, and Xander won't tell me. All I do know is that Kolt was supposed to take over for Matriarch, and then one day last year he became the black sheep and Xander got handed a position he didn't ask for. Whatever happened was bad enough that they nearly kicked Kolt out, which is a fate worse than death in their eyes, especially when he's a Legacy and one from Elizabeth I's line at that."

From what Adelaide could remember of Kolt before his family moved away from Atkin County, he'd had a bit of a wild streak, but what could he have done that was bad enough to nearly be kicked out of the Red Rose Society? "What's a Legacy?"

"A Legacy is a member of near direct descent from their Root. Only a select few people in the Red Rose Society can claim to be one. Xander and Kolt, me and Teddy and a few others in some different branches."

"If most of the Red Rose Society aren't direct descendants, then how are Kindred chosen for initiation?"

Charlie shrugged. "No one really knows how Kindred are selected, but it's done by the Enclave of Red Rose Society leaders and Matriarch. As far as I know, she makes the final decision and sends the letters."

"But you saw Matriarch's face at the gala." Adelaide shook her head. "She didn't choose me."

From the way things had unfolded upon her return from Revolutionary France and what she had learned about her mother, Adelaide knew she hadn't been sent that letter on accident. Someone wanted her there. She considered, not for the first time, what that really meant. Someone in the Red Rose Society knew something was different about her, perhaps even before Adelaide herself had known. But who? And just how much did they know?

They had stopped in front of a vintage boutique, the storefront window decorated in a series of faceless mannequins dressed in everything from Victorian ball gowns to seventies swimwear. The night bubbled with laughter and the bustle of people weaving in and out of shops and alleys, restaurants and nightclubs. Did they know the secrets their city held, soaked into the ground like rain? If they did, did they embrace them, letting lies light their lips as a barrier to the truth, or did they simply choose to forget?

Charlie leaned against the stone wall beside the window, and the gold in her hazel eyes shimmered in the electric lights that lined the sidewalk. Since the letter arrived, Adelaide had been asking herself who might have sent it, but maybe the better question was how? Colden could pick locks, Elise was resourceful, Xander and Charlie both had keys they could have used or had stolen from them. But of those people who immediately came to mind, only two of them knew her well enough to know she would need more of an incentive than just the letter to make her drop everything and fly to Scotland.

And while Xander was a master at wearing a mask, Adelaide had always been able to see through the cracks. When she showed him the article in that alley in Paris, he hadn't lied. His mother was his Achilles heel, and until Adelaide had suggested it, she could tell Xander had never considered the fire was anything but an accident.

That left the girl in front of her. The one who punched Wyatt Hudson in the face in fifth grade for making fun of Adelaide's lanky limbs. Who forgot her favorite color but knew the quieter she got, the more she needed to talk. Who refused to leave her side the night of the fire even when her tears dried up and she finally drifted off to sleep. "You know what, forget it. That's a question for another night. You said there was something you wanted to show me?"

Charlie pushed off the wall, letting their previous conversation drop. "It was this, actually." She opened the shop door, bell chiming as they crossed the threshold. "I've been wanting to take you here for years. I can never quite walk through it without hearing your voice as a running commentary in my head on the connection between the evolution of women's fashion and female activism."

Adelaide softened, a smile lighting her lips. "Well, it is a rather fascinating intersection. Come on."

Walking in felt like walking back in time. Now that she had actually time traveled, Adelaide felt she had the proper experience to make that comparison. Clothes and accessories spilled from every nook and cranny. Riding cloaks and hoop skirts transitioned into Mary Janes and skater skirts as

Adelaide and Charlie walked the rows and breathed in the fresh scent of lilacs and linen perfuming the air. Adelaide had expected a *trace* to go off like a flare gun the second she entered the boutique, but since the one she had hours earlier, that part of her had quieted. She could still feel it there, like a sixth sense, but it felt empty as a dried well waiting for rain to come replenish it. Still, she took care to touch things sparingly, not wanting to push her luck.

Try as she might to lose herself in the task at hand, Adelaide couldn't shake Matriarch's words. She had assumed the woman knew more than she was letting on. How could she not, given her position? Between the conversation Adelaide had heard in the corridor and what Matriarch had said after her last *trace*, Adelaide was certain the woman was hiding something. She just didn't know what.

Charlie pulled a dress from an antique wardrobe and held it to her frame. "What do you think about this one for the auction?"

"It's pretty, but I thought you weren't a big fan of green."

"I'm not, but it'll make your hair and freckles pop like poinsettias on a Christmas tree. Here." Charlie handed Adelaide the dress, draping it over her arms as she ushered her toward the dressing rooms. "Try this on."

Adelaide obliged, closing the curtains across the entrance of the room. She slipped out of her clothes and into the dress, the silky olive fabric cool on her skin. Heading barefoot out of the dressing room, she stood in front of the standing mirror beside it. It wasn't a dress she would have ever picked out for herself, but Charlie was right. Not only did it make her hair and freckles pop, it amplified the green in her hazel eyes. Thick straps hung off her shoulders, connecting in an elegant v that dipped just above her chest. The top half hugged the curves of her lengthy figure to the knee where it flared ever so slightly in a mermaid-style cut. It was a dress straight from Old Hollywood, more suited for Grace Kelly than her, but Adelaide couldn't help but admit she liked the way she felt in it—bold, confident and beautiful.

Charlie exited her dressing room in a long black and gold dress with twenties-style beading. She swept her curls to one side as she met Adelaide's eyes in the mirror. "Ad, you look stunning."

Adelaide smoothed her hands down the dress. "You don't think it's too much for an auction?"

Charlie shook her head. "Trust me. It's perfect."

Adelaide made to respond, but as she did, the muffled sound of arguing filtered from the back of the boutique. A door flew open, thudding against the wall. She stepped into the aisle to get a better view of the commotion and nearly collided with a rapidly retreating figure. Kolt skidded to a halt, hands in his pockets as he registered the girl in front of him. "Ad, uh, wow."

"See," Charlie said, a teasing smile on her lips. "He agrees with me. Stunning."

Adelaide felt a flush tinge her cheeks, probably also amplified by the green of the dress, but she ignored it. "Is everything okay?"

Kolt swallowed. "Yeah, just a little misunderstanding." He said it almost with a sigh, the hint of something underneath his words. Was it disappointment? "Anyway, I have to go. I'll see you guys later." With that, he left, the chime of the bell following him out.

Adelaide turned to Charlie and wondered what she made of the interaction. "What was that all about?"

"Beats me," Charlie said, slipping off a pair of heels she had tried on. "I stopped trying to puzzle out Kolt a long time ago."

Something about the look on his face as she watched him walk out struck her. It was the same look she wore every time she hit a dead end in her parents' case, spinning her wheels unsure where to go next. She thought about their detour to the coffee shop on their way to Holyrood and the file the man had slipped Kolt across the table. Was he really researching for a new novel or was it something more than that? The more she thought about it, the more it seemed to her like he was searching for something. But what?

18

FORGOTTEN

Crisp air chilled Adelaide's skin as she stepped out of the cab. It was late, the moon a round, bright glow in the sky when she reached the brick building that housed The Bean of Scots and Kolt's apartment. She hadn't planned to come, but as Charlie hailed them a cab to head back to headquarters, Adelaide knew she couldn't go back just yet. She wasn't sure why she felt compelled, but sometimes her feet carried her to places she needed to go before her mind knew exactly where that was or why. After seeing Charlie safely away, she'd signaled for a cab of her own and told the man at the wheel to just drive. He'd given her a quizzical look, but did as she asked, probably more than happy to let the meter run while she watched the world pass by outside the window. It wasn't until they neared the familiar turn that Adelaide knew where she needed to go. *The Bean of Scots.*

Adelaide figured if they locked anything, it would be the front, so she headed straight for the back entrance that she and Kolt had used when they stopped here before Holyrood. Gravel crunched beneath her feet as she rounded the side of the building. She could hear the muffled sounds of the city in the distance, but in the quiet off the beaten path, her own footsteps echoed louder than any other sound. Coffee grounds and vanilla scented the air, carried to her by a breeze that swirled dust on the street. It made her crave the hot drink Kolt had bought for her earlier or the rose tea Gideon continued to make for her during their chess games.

Adelaide didn't have to worry if Kolt was up. When she approached the back entrance, he was already there, silhouetted against the brick wall. A cigarette hung from his fingertips, the bright embers igniting a hot red as he took a drag. Hands in her jean pockets, Adelaide leaned a shoulder against the wall beside him. Kolt kept his eyes on the sky and blew out a breath, the smoke like a layer of mist as it left his lips. "What are you doing here, Ad?"

She let her head rest against the cool brick and wondered what the right answer to that question was. "I wanted to see if you were okay. You seemed pretty shaken when Charlie and I ran into you at the boutique."

Kolt let the cigarette fall to the ground and snuffed the flame beneath his foot. "I'm fine."

Adelaide scoffed. "I've used that line enough to know that it's a lie."

Kolt, his eyes cloaked in shadows, finally looked at her. She shivered, half from his gaze and half from the breeze that swept once again through the lot. Kolt's features softened as he ran a defeated hand across his brow. "Come on."

He pushed off from the wall and held the door for her. Adelaide stepped inside, welcoming the warmth and vanilla scent that was even stronger within the walls than it had been without. Kolt locked the door behind them and proceeded up the stairs. She followed, at ease as the familiar feel of worn floorboards creaked beneath her feet. At the top of the stairs, Kolt pushed open the door to his apartment. The room stretched out to their right, echoing the lengthy but shallow architecture of the coffee shop below. It was nice, a smooth blend of antique and grunge that somehow worked. The aroma of maple and sea salt wrapped around her as she moved deeper into the apartment. A record skipped on the turntable beside a leather chair, making Adelaide wonder how long Kolt had been standing outside before she got there.

Kolt made his way to the kitchen at the opposite end and tossed his keys into a bowl atop a small marble island. "Do you want a coffee? My last pot is almost out, but I can make another."

Adelaide slid onto a stool at the counter. "Do you have any tea?"

"Xander used to drink that crap too." He smirked, but it didn't quite reach his eyes. "I think I might still have a box here somewhere."

He rustled through the cabinets and emerged from the depths of one with an assorted box of tea. "Looks like all that's left is peppermint. Does that work?"

"I'm not surprised. I used to drink those for him because he didn't want to waste them."

Kolt dug two bags out of the box and put a kettle on the stove. "I'm not much for tea, but I don't think I can drink another cup of coffee tonight."

Adelaide didn't blame him and probably wouldn't have let him even if he'd tried. Outside, the darkness had hidden Kolt well, but inside the light gave everything away. Shadows darkened the skin beneath his eyes, and his hands trembled as he filled the mugs with hot water and slid one across to her.

She asked him, once again, the same question she had before. "Are you okay?"

Kolt was silent, the moment stretching on long enough that Adelaide wasn't sure he was going to answer until he finally spoke. "What happened at Holyrood?"

Adelaide swallowed her tea, the hot liquid scalding her throat. "What do you mean?"

"Before we left, in the room with Darnley's locket, did you—" he paused, choosing his next words carefully, "see anything?"

Adelaide set her mug down, wondering what their time at Holyrood had to do with her question. She met Kolt's gaze across the counter. The few feet of marble separating them might as well have been miles because in that moment she could tell that he knew. He knew about her *traces*. But even as the realization hit her, she couldn't get the truth to leave her lips. Instead, a simple, "Like what?" squeaked out instead.

He nodded slowly, as if her response was confirmation enough of what they both knew. "I have something you should see."

He rounded the counter and opened the door at the edge of the kitchen. Adelaide hesitated only a moment before following him across the threshold. Moonlight streamed in through the large window above his bed on the opposite wall. Kolt flipped the switch, chasing the dark away with the warm glow of an Edison bulb on the ceiling. She was just about to ask what he wanted to show her when her eyes found his desk. A series of books and journals coated its surface. Bunches of paper were stuck between their pages as placeholders, but what was on the desk wasn't nearly as interesting as what was above it. A massive cork board hung on the wall, nearly every inch plastered with newspaper clippings, printed articles and hand-written notes. Red string ran from push pin to push pin, telling a story Adelaide had a hard time deciphering.

"What is this?"

Kolt hesitated, but the words pushed past his lips. He spoke quickly, like he needed to get them out or wanted to before he changed his mind. "A few years ago, a girl named Sienna came to the Ancestral Gala as a Kindred, and like you, grandmother denied having sent her an invitation. When Sienna came back from the jump it was the first time anyone successfully brought an item back without it crumbling."

Adelaide stilled, her heart roaring in her ears. *Sienna.* The name stirred something in her mind until she realized it was the same one she'd seen the woman write in the ledger during her *trace*. A million questions raced in her mind, but she bit them back, afraid to speak before Kolt had finished.

"We became close, close enough for me to notice when she started acting off. Eventually, she told me she could see what she called *imprints.* She explained them as layers of history in an object or place. I saw it happen a few times. She got the same look on her face that you did at Holyrood." He fiddled with a button on his jean jacket, a sad frustration in his eyes. "I told her to consider telling grandmother, that maybe the Red Rose Society had resources or information that could help her figure out what she was seeing and why."

"What happened?" Adelaide asked, daring to hope that they did or that she could talk to Sienna.

"I don't know." Kolt shook his head as if he were trying to clear away cobwebs. "The rest of the story is blank. It only started coming back more, in bits and pieces, when you appeared with the earring unscathed."

Adelaide started pacing, her feet carrying her across the small room as she processed what Kolt was saying. "If Sienna brought something back before I did, why was everyone so surprised? Juniper and Matriarch made it seem like I was the first."

"To them, Sienna never existed. I don't understand it, but for me, she was there and then... nothing. It seems like I'm the only one who even remembers she was here at all. I mentioned her name a few times to people who knew her, and all I got was a blank stare."

"You're looking for her," Adelaide said, finally understanding the purpose of the corkboard and the desk spilled over with notes.

"Yeah, I thought I had a lead at the boutique, but it was just another dead end. All I know right now is that I need to find her. I think she's in trouble, and it's all my fault."

19

CHASING GHOSTS

———

Everything within Adelaide screamed that this was a bad idea. But despite the mental war waging within her, her feet continued forward, already resigned to the fact that she was running out of time and options. She'd replayed the last *trace* she had in her head. Over and over again she had tried to make sense of the scene and the man within it, but every time she had come to the same conclusion. The man was Father Jude. It didn't make sense that the man from the *trace* was the same man from the graveyard, but there was only one way she would ever know.

Adelaide walked into the gym. The sharp scent of sweat and rubber seemed to radiate from the walls, having soaked into the pores of the sleek flooring. Thick wooden beams criss-crossed the ceiling above, running parallel to the crisp lines of the L-shaped room. Aside from a few pairs of figures fencing on the side, the gym was relatively empty. Though a larger gathering would have meant a better chance for anonymity, it would have also meant more wandering ears tuned to a conversation not meant for them.

She found the boxing ring near the far corner of the gym, lined on either side by a series of heavyweight bags suspended along the wall. A lone figure stood at the bag farthest from her. His hands were wrapped in linen, but devoid of gloves or other padding to soften the vicious blows he was landing repeatedly on the bag. Teo's back was bare, leaving visible a series of thickened scars along the contours of his tanned skin like the scattered stars of a constellation. Bouncing on his feet as his fists fell fast and furious, he circled the bag. He paused, resetting his position. His eyes clocked her watching him, and he turned back to the bag as she approached.

Adelaide's eyes fell on Teo's chest. Scrawled across its surface, just above his heart, was the elegant loops of a woman's handwriting inked on his skin. *Someday they'll go down together.* Something about the line felt familiar, teasing the edge of her mind until she remembered it was a line from Bonnie Parker's journal. The thud of a punch jolted Adelaide from her thoughts. She pulled her eyes from his chest, forcing them to look anywhere else, and took a breath, stealing herself for the words to follow. "I need you to do something for me."

Teo scoffed as he released a jab, chains jangling from the impact. "And here I thought it was the pleasure of my company you were after. Pity."

"Believe me, if I was looking for the pleasure of someone's company, you would be far down on that list."

Teo swung his fist in a hook and grabbed the bag to steady it. A sheen coated his skin as he caught his breath, a smirk teasing the corner of his lips. "But I would be on it."

"That's not what I meant—" Adelaide shook her head. "That's beside the point. Can you arrange a meeting with Father Jude?"

Teo's head shot up from unwrapping his hands. Curiosity lit in his eyes. "What do you want with Father Jude?"

"Does it matter?"

"I guess not."

"So will you do it?"

Teo pulled a towel from the bench along the wall and rubbed it behind his neck. "I'll think about it." With that, he tossed it at Adelaide and walked away.

She caught it and quickly balled it up. "Hey," she shouted after him and threw it at his back. The towel bounced off him, falling in a crumpled pile to the floor. "That's it? Where are you going?"

Teo turned to retrieve the towel and slung it over his shoulder. "To shower. You're welcome to come, but you'll have to bring your own towel. I'm not sharing."

Though Adelaide hated to admit it, chess with Gideon was something she was starting to look forward to. They had gotten into a routine of facing off across the polished mahogany board every couple of days. As it stood, she was currently in the lead. It felt strange walking past the corridor that held his office, but he had run into her earlier with a remorseful apology that he would have to cancel tonight's game. So instead, Adelaide headed back to her room. She scanned in, opened the door, and was greeted by the sweet scent of rose from the candle Elise had picked up in the city. Adelaide had thought it was a little too on the nose to burn a rose-scented candle in the Red Rose Society, but the irony of it was precisely why Elise had bought in the first place.

She started to kick off her shoes but froze as she took in the sight before her. A white box with a crudely tied bow atop it sat at the end of her bed. The box itself would have been enough to stop her in her tracks, but the figure seated beside it had truly made her pause. Teo perched on the edge, his head bent over a book. Adelaide flicked her eyes to the empty nightstand where one of her mother's journals had been and back to the leather cover between his hands. Heat flared on her neck as an invisible hand tied her stomach in knots. She ripped the journal from his hands and clutched it to her chest like it was a life raft and she was drowning. "What are you doing?"

Teo opened his mouth to respond, a sharp response on his tongue, but as he met her gaze his features softened. She could see herself reflected in his dark eyes. Though anger coursed through her like a tide, the girl who looked back at her looked small and frightened. "I'm sorry. I was waiting for you and... I didn't realize what it was."

Adelaide knew it was a perfectly logical explanation. No markings on the outside of the journal signified it was anything other than an average book. But it wasn't an average book and logic had left the moment Adelaide had seen the journal in Teo's hands. "Did you get enough information or did you want me to leave while you rifle through the rest?"

Teo's eyes narrowed. "I shouldn't have touched your things in the first place but—"

"You're right," Adelaide cut him off. "You shouldn't have."

"You know what," Teo said, squeezing his fists as he sidled up to her. "I didn't mean to read your mother's journal, but I did learn one thing from it."

Adelaide refused to move, even though they were mere inches from each other. "And what's that?"

"You and I," he said, his gaze unwavering, "are more alike than you think."

"I am nothing like you."

"Yeah?" Teo tilted his head. "Then why are you here if not to chase ghosts?"

"If you think you know me so well, you tell me since you don't just chase ghosts. Everywhere you go you make them."

Teo recoiled as if she had just slapped him. She hadn't meant to press on a wound so similar to her own, but as the words left her mouth images of Barrow flashed in her mind: the crack of a gun, the spread of blood across her shirt, the shock on her face as she fell over the side of the platform and the barrel of a gun, gripped tightly between Teo and Colden's hands as they grappled for it.

Teo's eyes flared as his jaw clenched in anger. From the moment she met him, Adelaide understood Teo to be a lot of things—mysterious, charming, tough—but it wasn't until this very moment that she had come to realize he was something else too, dangerous.

An eerie calm settled on his features as he thrust something small into the palm of her hand. He leaned in, his voice hard but edged in sadness. "You have no idea." He stepped back. "I believe your father had a friend who can help me with that. Get him to run a test, off the books, and I'll arrange a meeting with Father Jude."

Teo walked to the door, and his hands poised above the knob as he turned back toward her. "Oh, and this one is a tradeoff, tit for tat. You still owe me. And I always collect."

With that final word of parting, Teo left. It wasn't until Adelaide heard the door click into place behind her that she let out a shaky breath. Her hands shook from adrenaline, and as much as she hated to admit it, from fear. She unfurled her fingers to find a small glass vial in her hand. Inside was a grouping of several dark human hairs. She gasped, holding the vial as far away from herself as she could, trying to resist the impulse to let it drop from her fingers and shatter on the ground.

She thought of Teo cutting silently through the water on the lake in the dark of night, of the scars on his back and the flame in his eyes only moments ago. Asking him for help back in Paris, like she had again a few days ago, had seemed her best option, her only option. She could only hope learning the truth would be worth the risk of what she knew she had to do with the vial. And with whatever Teo needed when he cashed in his favor.

20

TRACES

———

Mary brought the goblet to her lips, a flush tingeing her cheeks as she sipped the dark liquid inside. The murmur of voices in the great hall built to a crescendo, breaking like a wave against the stone walls. She stifled a giggle and motioned for a servant to refill her cup as a lively melody filled the air.

A long table stretched before her toward the back of the hall. Adorned in plates of roast duck and bowls of figs, its dark surface was ripe with color from a wide variety of food and drink. Only moments ago, every chair had been filled. Now, many sat empty as their former occupants were deep in the throes of a waltz on the dance floor. She could see Francis, dancing with one of her ladies. When the song ended, he bowed to her and passed her hand to the next gentleman. As the minstrels readied for another song, Francis found her across the room. A soft smile lit his lips as he walked off the dance floor and to her chair.

"I have a surprise for you." He bent and kissed her hand, drawing her up beside him.

This time, Mary didn't suppress her laugh. "Oh, really? And what might that be?"

A mischievous glint lit his eyes as the doors of the hall swung open, cutting off the music. Mary watched in awe as several grand ships of dark wood and gold rolled into the room. Their sails billowing as if tossed by an ocean breeze. She grabbed his hand and ran to the nearest one, the Valois and Stuart crests painted side by side on its hull.

Francis placed his hands on her waist and lifted her over the side. Mary lay back on the silk pillows arranged on the deck. Her eyes found the clouds of the painted ceiling above as they had when she and Francis were young. If she closed her eyes, she could almost imagine they were alone, adrift at sea. No titles, no duties, just sky and sea and the dark between stars. Mary was born to be a queen but sometimes let herself wonder what it would be like to have that kind of freedom, to sail and explore the way traders did, to chart her own course.

Francis settled beside her. The warm vanilla scent of his youth still clung to him. The scent brought her back to childhood. The weight of his eyes was as familiar as his scent. She opened her own eyes to his smile. The light above his head formed a golden halo around his fair hair as his gaze dipped to her mouth.

He reached to tuck a strand of flaming hair behind her ear. The graze of his finger against her cheek ignited a heat just as bold within her and yet, a sliver of something lingered cold. She stilled.

The light in his eyes darkened as a frown etched the corner of his mouth. "Did I do something wrong?"

Mary's chest tightened as she weighed her words. She loved Francis. He was memories of tag on the palace lawn and quiet glances across the dining table, secret sword lessons in the dead of night and shared burdens under the stars. But Mary knew in her heart of hearts that loving someone and being in love were two vastly different things. Duty had bound them since she was five years old. Despite being a queen, choice was one thing she seldom had. Marriage to Francis wasn't her choice, but what if love could be? From their shared youth, they were bound by more than duty. She refused to believe the bonds they shared couldn't grow to something more in time.

Francis moved to pull his hand away, but she caught it to her cheek. It was warm beneath her own. "I love it."

He sighed, a gentleness in his eyes that made her want to wrap her arms around him. "Mary, I'm not fooled into thinking love is the reason our stories have become one today. But maybe, in time, we can find it together along the way as we write this next chapter."

She nestled her cheek against his palm. "I'd like that."

Francis smiled and slid his hand to cup her head, dipping his to meet her lips in a tender kiss. It wasn't passionate, swoon worthy or earth shaking, but it held a promise, and for Mary, in that moment, it was enough.

21

CLOCKS, RINGS AND OTHER BROKEN THINGS

———

After weeks of preparation, the evening of the auction finally arrived. Adelaide and Charlie had gotten there early, ready to check off the rows of names on Charlie's clipboard as the guests began to roll in. The murmur of voices built in the room as the sun began its descent. Rays of light filtered through the long windows. They coated the crowd in layers of orange and gold like flames. Waiting for the event to start, guests mingled with each other among the scatter of cocktail tables in the back of the room.

Of all the elements of this affair, the guest list had been Charlie's proudest achievement. Even more impressive than the names, crisp and clean on paper, were their real-life counterparts quickly filling the room. Politicians and other men of distinction in pressed suits and dark ties flashed kilowatt smiles in greeting as they shook hands, slipping secrets on scraps of paper between their palms. Their wives and girl-friends in gem-colored dresses and pearls gossiped amongst each other, laughter on their lips as they leaned in close and kissed one another's cheeks, searching for the perfume that clung to their partners' clothing late at night. Young and old, celebrity and millionaire, the one thing they held in common was the thick bulge of a checkbook in their jacket pocket.

Adelaide swiped the sweat at her brow as another couple walked through the doors. Charlie greeted them and crossed their names off before sending them to Adelaide and shifting her attention to the next guests in line. Adelaide smiled, but the woman brushed past her and melded with the crowd by the bar. She didn't stop to bother a glance at Adelaide or confirm if her date for the night followed behind her.

"You'll have to excuse Lorena," the man said, his dark eyes and grey suit stark against his olive skin. "She's nice enough, given the chance, but you don't want to get between her and a gin martini."

"I'll keep that in mind," Adelaide handed the man his assigned auction paddle. "Enjoy your evening."

His gaze swept the room, a smile on his face as he spotted something in the crowd, though Adelaide couldn't tell what. "I believe I will." With that, he walked away in the opposite direction of the bar.

Adelaide shifted the dress on her frame, but it fell back in place, smooth over the bend and curves of her figure. She had felt beautiful earlier, but the moment had passed, leaving her with the strong desire to head back to her room and throw on an oversized t-shirt and leggings. Though she had left the dress behind at the store, she had opened the box left on her bed in Teo's absence and pulled the silky material from the wrappings. A note was nestled amidst the olive fabric, inked on the cardstock as if typed by a typewriter, but it simply read, *To Adelaide*, with no additional clues as to who had sent it.

She'd put on the dress and a light layer of make-up, and with Charlie's help, swept and pinned her crimson curls into an elegant waterfall that fell full and loose down the front of her left shoulder with a few twists and braids concealed within. Her naturally tall height negated her need for heels, lest she wanted to tower above the crowd more than she already did, and the cut of the dress allowed for her high-tops to be worn beneath without the risk of being seen.

She wondered if Xander had picked up on the fact that she still wore them nearly every day, despite the weird air between them, and that she had worn them even when he was an ocean away. As if conjured by her thoughts, Xander now stood before her in a navy-blue suit. Golden cufflinks glistened at his wrists, and his normally free hair was gelled back, erasing the gentle waves that usually tousled it.

He hesitated before leaning in to kiss her cheek. His proximity wrapped her in a warm cinnamon scent that reminded Adelaide of the changing of seasons, of the shift from summer to fall that brought with it both decay and newness in equal measure. "Never thought I'd catch you in a dress this long."

Adelaide started to respond, but Xander's father walked in. "Come, Xander. There's someone I wish to introduce you to."

Xander's smile faltered as his eyes found hers again. "I have to go but promise you'll find me later tonight. Okay?"

Adelaide promised and watched him walk off with his father.

"That should be the last of them," Charlie said, running back through the names on her list. The baby blue of her dress brought out the pale grey in her eyes. Threads of silver glinted on the bodice in the form of tiny flowers that winked like the crystals in the chandeliers overhead. "I've got to go check on some last-minute details. Why don't you go mingle a bit?"

Charlie left, leaving Adelaide to scan the crowd for a familiar face. She spotted Colden among a group of men. She recognized several as politicians she had seen on TV and in the newspaper. Though Colden's passion for art ran deep, Adelaide knew he dreamed of one day running for office. She wondered if that was what the Red Rose Society had promised him, accessibility to the very people who could help him turn that dream into a reality. Elise stood beside him, deep in conversation with a blonde-haired woman in an elegant evening gown. Elise smiled as she spoke, but it didn't quite reach her eyes, her mind probably on the fact that it was Colden's final night in headquarters. Elise had shared with her the other day that the Red Rose Society was sending Colden on assignment already. She wasn't sure what the task was, but she did know it would have him stationed in another European country for an indefinite amount of time.

As theirs didn't appear to be a conversation she could easily slip into, Adelaide let her gaze continue to wander. The woman from earlier, Lorena, still sat at the bar beside a man with dark hair and a tailored suit that looked more expensive than the thick gold watch on his wrist. Though Lorena and the man didn't acknowledge each other, the familiarity in their body language made Adelaide wonder if they knew one another. Their knees were a breadth away from touching beneath the oak countertop. He smoked a cigar, pulling drags from it as he spoke to a man on the other side of him. She chatted with Kolt who stood behind the bar. He met Adelaide's gaze and mouthed the words *nice dress* before throwing a playful wink her way as he strained another martini into Lorena's empty glass.

Other Kindred intermixed with the interesting array of guests. Though she tried not to, Adelaide couldn't help but notice Teo was not among them. She thought about his comment the other day, about her chasing ghosts. Maybe he was right. The deeper into the Red Rose Society she got, the farther away the truth seemed to slip. Despite now being in a world her parents had once claimed as their own, she couldn't see them in the fancy dresses and finery, the technology and time travel or the secrets that seemed to dangle from everyone's lips.

She was just starting to wonder what other secrets her parents had kept from her when Gideon approached. "You look lovely, my dear. A spitting image of Anna. Don't you think?"

He addressed the latter half of his sentence to the man beside him. Adelaide recognized him from the sign-in line, the one who had come with Lorena.

"Without a doubt. I knew there was something about you when I saw you earlier. I don't know how I missed it before."

A momentary silence settled in as Gideon realized he hadn't introduced them. "Oh, Adelaide, this is Luka La Torre. Luka, this is my niece, Adelaide."

He nodded at her, extending his hand. She shook it. "Nice to meet you, Mr. La Torre."

"Call me Luka, please. I need a few more grey hairs on my head before I start going by Mr. La Torre."

From the looks of him, Luka didn't appear to be that old. If Adelaide had to venture a guess, she'd place him around Gideon's age, a few years younger than her parents had been.

Matriarch materialized beside Gideon, the folds of her dress wrapping her in sleek layers of dark silk and silver. "I see Gideon managed to get you on the list after all. I guess they'll let in any scum off the street these days."

Luka smirked. "It's good to see you too, Maggie."

Maggie. It was the same name the man's voice in the hallway had called Matriarch the night Adelaide had stumbled upon the hidden room Xander claimed as his artist hideaway. The man's face had been obscured by shadows, but could it have been Luka she heard that night?

Matriarch ignored him. If it wasn't beneath her, she probably would have rolled her eyes. She pulled the drink from

Gideon's hand as he brought it to his mouth and set it on the tray of a passing waiter. "That will have to wait. I need to borrow you momentarily."

Gideon looked at her, his hand still suspended mid motion and formed around the drink that was no longer in it. "This is a social gathering, Margaret. Does it physically pain you to enjoy yourself every once in a while?"

She narrowed her eyes at him. "Markus Thornbey has developed an interest in sailing. I thought you could tell him of your most recent excursion."

Only a moment passed before Gideon responded, but in that small span of time there seemed to be an unspoken communication between the two of them. "Very well." To Adelaide he added, "I'll see you later, kid. Don't think I forgot about our game. I plan on making quite the comeback."

Adelaide watched the two of them slip out of the room. Moments later, a trickle of other men followed, excusing themselves from their current conversations with other guests to slip away undetected. First Xander's father exited, then Charlie's, and then a third man who Adelaide assumed was Markus Thornbey.

"If I didn't know any better, I'd say they were up to something." Luka watched them, too, his eyes glinting like crystal. "But then again, who here isn't?"

Adelaide had been so focused on Matriarch and Gideon she hadn't realized Luka was still beside her. He took a sip of his drink, eyeing her above the glass with a knowing gaze that practically begged her to ask. "What do you know about it?"

Luka swirled his scotch, the movement clinking the ice cube against the glass. "Gideon is in a bit of hot water. Apparently, his trip around the world didn't prove to be as fruitful as his beloved society had hoped."

If what Luka said was true and Gideon had failed to find another source of Queen's Blood, the Red Rose Society still needed the gem for time travel. Would they send him back out in search of more?

Adelaide was about to ask Luka what else he knew when he continued, "But enough about him. I want to know about you. How does Anna have a daughter I don't know about?"

In the wake of Matriarch's sudden appearance, Adelaide had almost forgotten what Gideon said earlier and the familiarity in the way he spoke to Luka and about her mother. "You knew my mother?"

He nodded. "I did. For a time, we were quite close. I was sad to hear of her passing. And your father's too, of course."

Adelaide felt a lump form in her throat. It had been a while since she'd cried about her parents. Even a year later, she still found herself oscillating between periods of time when she was doing okay and others when a fresh wave of grief hit out of nowhere, spurred by the smallest of things: a mother and daughter out to lunch, a family walking along the beach, watching Charlie interact with her own mother. All the little things most people didn't see as blessings until they no longer had them. "Thank you."

Adelaide had so many questions she wanted to ask Luka. Somehow, it felt easier asking them of a total stranger than of Gideon or even Juniper. Unfortunately, her questions would have to wait because the static feedback of a microphone pierced the white noise of chatter in the hall.

"Sorry," Charlie laughed, standing on stage before the crowd. "I just wanted to thank you all so much for being here and to thank Matriarch as well for her willingness to donate half of the proceeds earned from tonight's auction to Harvard's Center for Marine Biology. We have some awesome items going up on the block tonight, so make sure you grab any last-minute drinks or hors d'oeuvres and get your paddle-raising arms ready because we'll be kicking things off in the next few minutes."

"Well, Adelaide, it's been a pleasure. I have to go wrangle Lorena from the bar, but I'm sure we'll be seeing each other again soon." Luka left, taking whatever answers he might have been able to provide with him.

Seeing as the auction was about to start, Adelaide figured she might as well grab a seat, but as she moved toward the chairs at the front of the room, she felt a firm hand grasp her arm. She whipped around, finding herself face to face with Teo. His eyes were wild but laced with an emotion Adelaide had never seen him show before, fear. "What did he want?"

Her eyes flicked from his hand on her arm and back to his face as his grip tightened. "Let go of me."

Teo looked at his hand around her arm as if he had just noticed it was still there. He let go and took a step back, repeating his question. "What did he want?"

"Luka?" she asked, wondering why on earth Teo cared. "Nothing, we were just talking."

Teo shook his head and dropped his voice. "There is no 'just talking' with Luka La Torre. The charisma and good manners are all an act. The center of his attention is not a place you want to be."

Adelaide crossed her arms. "Funny, Elise said the same thing about you."

A muscle in Teo's jaw twitched, but he let the comment slide. "You don't know who he is. Do you?"

"Should I?"

"Luka La Torre is a notorious mobster. The only other mob family alive that can hold a candle to his wealth, influence, and abilities is mine. He's responsible for the deaths of enough of my family, friends and—" Teo halted, flustered. "He's dangerous. Just stay away from him."

If what Teo said was true, why did Gideon associate with him? Another question pulled at the back of her mind, even more concerning than the first. Why had her mother? Luka said they were close at one point. Did she know at the time all the terrible things he had done and was capable of? "Fine, I'll stay away."

Teo nodded, relaxing a bit, but the ghost of something in his eyes still lingered under the surface. "Alright." He cleared his throat. "Did you send the vial to your dad's friend?"

Teo didn't need to elaborate. She'd put two and two together when she realized what was in the vial. She'd done what he asked and called Dr. Anderson, her father's colleague. He was a biological scientist who worked with and researched DNA. He also sequenced it. Though she didn't exactly know what Teo wanted with it, she figured the latter ability was of most interest to him. Why else would he ask her to send him the hair? She doubted it was to know the chemical properties contained in each strand.

"I did. He said it could take a little longer due to the water damage, but he should be able to get the results back within the next few days." She bit her lip, wondering if she should press further. "Are you going to tell me whose hair is in the vial and why you need it sequenced on the down low and not by a secret society you're a member of who also happens to specialize in DNA?"

"Aren't you the one who added the 'no questions asked' clause to your deal?"

"That was for the original deal. You made it clear this one was a swap, so 'no questions asked' doesn't apply here." Adelaide raised her chin. "Given the fact that human body parts are involved, don't you think I have a right to at least know whose it is?"

"Figured you would have worked that one out by now."

Adelaide had a suspicion. Between Teo's late night trips across the loch, the hair, and what Dr. Anderson had said about water damage, there was only one person it could belong to. "Barrow."

Teo's look all but confirmed it.

"But why run her DNA? She's dead. You were there. We watched her die."

Teo rubbed the back of his neck with his hand. "Not exactly. We watched her get shot and fall over the edge, but we never actually saw her die. Barrow has a small tattoo on the side of her foot that matched with her sister. I checked the body in the boat and there was no tattoo on it."

Adelaide remembered Teo standing by the boat, head bent as if in prayer. She knew now that he had been checking for the tattoo, but it was dark that night. Adelaide knew what it was like to see things that weren't there or in Teo's case, not see things that were there. Grief does strange things to a person. He could have easily missed the tattoo even if it was right there in front of his face. Adelaide hoped for Teo's sake Barrow was still alive somewhere, but either way, they wouldn't know until Dr. Anderson got back to her. "I'll get you the results as soon as I can."

Teo nodded, seemingly content with her answer. "You know the top floor of the library, the alcove beneath the dome?"

It seemed to be the place she practically lived these days. "Yeah, I know it."

"You'll find a hidden room behind the bust of Apollo. Make your way up there right after the bidding and knock on the wall five times. Father Jude will be waiting for you."

"What did you tell him?"

Teo looked at her like the answer was obvious. "That you wanted to talk to him."

"Did he say anything?"

"Nothing more than I just told you." He narrowed his eyes at her. "But he didn't seem all that surprised by your request—" Teo trailed off.

Adelaide followed his eyes to Luka, Lorena, and the man that had sat beside her at the bar. He was short and toned, his olive skin and navy suit not unlike Teo's. The three of them appeared to be arguing, but Adelaide was having a hard time figuring out who was against who as words seemed to be tossed around each of them equally.

Teo rubbed a hand across his tired face. "I have to go before someone ends up dead."

She watched him walk away, and though he left her with urgency, every step he took toward Luka and the others seemed to be slower than the last. At last, he joined the argument, ushering them to the side so as to avoid attention, but people were already starting to notice them. Adelaide thought fists would start to fly, but the screech of the microphone pierced the air again, signaling it was time to start the bidding. Teo pushed Luka and the man toward chairs on opposite sides of the room. Lorena rushed to follow Luka, but Teo stepped in her path. They talked in hushed, sharp tones, but Adelaide couldn't tell what they were saying. Finally, Lorena pushed past him and slid into the seat beside Luka.

Teo stood there, still, for what felt like hours, but could only have been a matter of seconds. He turned slowly, as if carrying the weight of the world on his shoulders, his eyes connecting with hers. It was only a moment before he looked away and found a seat amongst the other guests, but in that brief moment, he seemed to share with her all his secrets at once. They were finally there, hovering on the surface instead of lingering in the depths of him, and though the gaze held a thousand secrets, it lacked the words to truly tell her what they were.

Adelaide took her own seat in the back row, squeezing into one of the only available chairs left. The bidding started, but she tuned it out, lost in the plethora of thoughts swirling around in her head. What exactly had Gideon been doing for the last ten years around the world as he searched for Queen's Blood? What was the mysterious meeting with Markus Thornbey about? Did the vial really contain Barrow's hair? And what had just happened between Luka, Lorena, and the other man?

As her thoughts swirled like a whirlpool, a senator won a campaign button from George Washington's re-election, a rising music star won a key from Beethoven's piano and a billionaire philanthropist won a chunk of rock that was part of the Sphinx's nose. More items came and went as the guests threw money around like rain. Adelaide couldn't help but feel a little off-put about the whole thing. Sure, half the money was going to a worthy cause, but shouldn't these items be in museums? How could the Red Rose Society preach protecting the past yet auction off pieces of it?

The auctioneer brought another item forward. It was a small mantel clock, carved from a deep cherry wood that glowed red in the light. The man dictated the corresponding page in their catalogs to flip to and gave them a moment to read about the item. Adelaide scanned the entry as he continued to tell them it had once belonged to Al Capone. She searched for Teo, but the seat he had previously occupied was empty.

"Bid on the clock." Teo's voice came from behind her. "I don't care what you have to do or how high it goes, I need you to get it."

Adelaide had never heard him use the word *need* before. "What? Why? I don't even have a paddle."

"Here." He pushed a paddle into her hand. "Do this, and I'll forget you owe me."

She didn't have time to think, let alone respond as the auctioneer started the bidding. A few people raised their paddles, Adelaide included, as the price continued to climb. The higher it went, the fewer people remained until Adelaide found herself bidding against Luka.

He threw his paddle up again with speed, and Adelaide went to match it, but before she could, a crack slit the room. Time seemed to slow again as it had in the library, and Adelaide watched as a fissure made its way across the frescoes overhead. Dust rained down on the guests, but as quick as it happened, it snapped back in place. The ringing in her ears was steadily replaced by the auctioneer's word. "Sold, to the man in the fine blue suit." She looked to Luka, who threw a sly grin in her direction, but it went over her head to Teo. She turned to stammer an apology, but Teo was already across the room and slipping through the door.

22

THE MARKS WE LEAVE BEHIND

———

Adelaide ran out the door of the auction hall. The padding of her feet on the stone replaced the trill of the auctioneer's voice as she searched the surrounding corridors for Teo. She wanted to apologize for losing the clock to Luka, but the raw pain on Teo's face when he left told her it wasn't something he would easily forgive. It shook her to see him break like he did, as if he had shattered so many times, he could no longer hold his pieces together. Adelaide sighed, giving up her search. Not wanting to venture back into the chaos of the auction, she followed the familiar path to the library.

The hidden door was right where Teo had said it would be, at least the statue guarding it was. It sat on a wooden pedestal, nestled into an alcove at the far end of the stacks in the upper portion of the library. Whoever had carved it was greatly skilled, working with the natural veins of grey in the pale stone so they reflected human veins along each of the bust's temples. Its eyes, in a similar manner, were carved around an area of variation in color, giving them an almost pale blue hue to their appearance.

Adelaide raised her hand to knock. She hesitated, remembering what Teo had said about rapping five times. Was she supposed to just knock like normal or tap it out in a rhythm of some sort? Figuring Father Jude would hear it either way, she chose a wall beside the statue and knocked five times in quick succession. The sound echoed off the hard surfaces of the shelves. Just when she was about to try again, the wall beside her swung inward. Cool air released from inside the passage, brushing over her bare shoulders and sending a chill down her spine. Adelaide stepped inside as the panel slid closed behind her.

In the near blackness, she could see a faint light a few yards ahead. She quickened her pace, a sense of panic creeping in as the walls closed in on either side, mere inches from her. Though there was no smell of smoke, it wrapped around her, clouding her vision as the weight of something heavy settled on her chest. A hand reached for her, pulling her out of the darkness and into the faint glow of light at the end of the passage.

Her breath came fast and heavy as she crossed the threshold of the tunnel into a small room. Confused about what she had just experienced, she cast her gaze back down the passage. It felt like a *trace* in the way it unfolded around her, but unlike her *traces*, she hadn't been touching anything to spark it. Was she so out of control that her *traces* no longer needed a catalyst to start them or was this something different all together? While what she usually saw in her *traces* felt real in the sense that Adelaide knew what she was seeing had actually happened in the past, whatever she had just seen felt real in a whole different way, more like a memory than a *trace*.

As her heart slowed, Adelaide took in the small room. Drop cloths covered the few pieces of furniture still standing. Dust, drifting lazily upward like smoke from an extinguished flame, wafted from the rug as her feet fell onto it. Through the haze, she fixated on the man across from her.

Father Jude looked exactly as she remembered—tall, thin and wrapped in folds of cloth and shadow. He was clean shaven and youthful, but his eyes hid a thousand stories belonging to the ages. His voice was firm but kind as he spoke. "I'm afraid we don't have long, Adelaide. I took a risk coming here, and there are matters I must soon return to. But I must admit, I am curious as to what has you seeking me out."

Adelaide froze, the words poised on her tongue, dangerously close to the edge, but still, she bit them back. What could she say that wouldn't make her sound crazy or elicit the same look from Father Jude that Sheriff Dawson and many others had given her? She wasn't even sure if he could help. She was operating on a hunch from a several-hundred-year-old inkwell and pen. Maybe she was crazy. Adelaide bit her lip. "I've been seeing things."

Father Jude raised an eyebrow. Clearly, she was off to a great start, but how else was she supposed to explain her *traces*. She took a breath, starting again. "You know how you walk through an old building and you can almost feel the people who walked there before you, see them around you as they were in the past?"

He nodded. "Go on."

"Well, I think I've—" she paused. "I think I've actually been seeing them."

"What do you mean?"

"Sometimes, when I touch an object with history, a scene unfolds around me. Like I'm actually there watching it in real time." Adelaide shook her head understanding how crazy she sounded. "Does that even make sense?"

"It does actually. I had a girl, not too long ago, tell me the same thing. While I don't understand it completely, I will tell you exactly what I told her. We all have secrets to hide and stories to tell. Objects are no different. Sometimes, when we die, the things we leave behind must tell our stories for us. It seems to me a story is out there waiting to be told and you are the only one who can uncover it."

"But why? How?"

"I don't know why. That is something you'll have to discover on your own. But as for how, my suggestion would be to listen. Everything hums with a story of the marks we leave behind, waiting for the right people to come along so they can share them. The next time these moments happen, tune out the noise of other stories and search for the one that calls loudest to you."

As strange as Father Jude's advice sounded, somehow, it made sense to her. And while Adelaide still didn't have all the answers, she had a starting point. "You won't tell anyone. Will you?"

"No," he said, resting a hand on her shoulder. "Nor should you unless you are certain they can be trusted. Stories are powerful things, and many will go to great lengths to make sure some remain untold."

Father Jude removed his hand and gave her a final nod in farewell. She thanked him for his help as he walked past her back through the tunnel. Though he seemed to believe her and provided advice, Adelaide hadn't told him about her most recent *trace*, the one that may or may not be of him or one of his ancestors. She wasn't sure what kept her from telling him, especially when she had revealed the truth of her *traces*, but at least for now, she kept the secret to herself hoping it would one day be a story she could tell and not one left behind to be told for her.

With Father Jude gone, Adelaide could see herself in the warped mirror on the wall behind where he had stood. Her reflection gazed back, distorted by time and decay that had been concealed in the walls. As she watched herself in the mirror, her mind snapped back to their conversation, a line floating to the surface of her thoughts. *I had a girl, not too long ago, tell me the same thing.*

She whipped around and ran back down the tunnel, straight through the hidden door and out onto the top floor of the library. Her eyes scanned the area, frantically searching for Father Jude, but he was gone. She swept her hair to the side, wondering how she could have missed it. She'd been so focused on the *traces* themselves that she glossed right over his words, but she felt a spark of hope ignite inside her as she came to the realization of what they could mean. She wasn't the only one.

23

SPARK THE FLAME

OCTOBER 23, 1862
RICHMOND, VIRGINIA

Once again, Adelaide found herself stepping down into another era. This time, instead of the greenery of early June, October claimed the landscape. The unusually warm weather had frozen the trees in a limbo state. Leaves still clung to the branches in an array of crisp oranges and browns, suspended in the moment before they'd fall to the ground and give way to winter.

Adelaide gripped her skirt in her hands to keep it from snagging on stray branches as they left the grove. Though Teo and Mikaelson wore a variation of the same clothing they had before, ERMA had suggested a different outfit for Adelaide this time. She was more than happy to leave the hoop skirt and corset behind, trading them and the dress for a more practical olive-green drop skirt and cream-colored blouse.

They followed the path out of the clearing and into the city. The market still bustled with activity, but the patrons had a more urgent energy. No longer were they strolling casually through, laughing and jesting with one another. Their steps were purposeful, their purchases limited to necessities. They kept their heads down, eyes focused on the goal of food on their table and clothes on their backs.

Though it was a far cry from the chaos of the French Revolution, Adelaide could sense the same tense atmosphere that had hung over Paris like a fog. Over a year had passed for Richmond between the first time Adelaide had walked its streets in the past and now. The war was still raging, already having lasted longer than anyone thought it would. And at this point, it wasn't even half over.

"I know I'm not bad on the eyes, but why is everyone staring at me?" Teo asked, meeting the glares of those who watched him as they walked by.

Whatever had come over him at the auction was gone or well-hidden, seeing he was in his normal spirits.

"Because you're an able-bodied man not in a uniform," Adelaide replied.

Teo grinned, an irritating smirk plastered on his lips. "You think I'm able bodied?"

She turned to him, her voice low and sharp. "They do. And they're wondering why their men are out there fighting and dying while you're strolling the local market alive and in one piece. Try to show a little tact for them and what they're going through. They don't have the luxury of leaving like we do."

Anger flared behind Teo's eyes, but it was quickly replaced with acceptance. "You're right. I'm sorry."

Adelaide nodded. "Just keep your head down and try not to draw too much attention."

It was easier said than done. The only way Teo could possibly stand out more was if he'd worn a Union uniform. Between his bronze skin and weathered clothes, it was a wonder if they passed someone who didn't stare. Not to mention he was one of only a few men in the market, save for Mikaelson, whose Confederate uniform spared him the same ire, a few of the vendors, and an old man on a bench reading a newspaper.

The man crumpled the paper and threw it to the ground. "Damn Yankees!"

Adelaide didn't need to purchase a paper of her own this time to understand the man's reaction. Dr. Jameson had shared with her a printed replica yesterday when he'd told her to prepare for another trip. It read October 23, 1862, and featured a string of articles on Union victories and prisoner releases. The Union could now count on two hands the number of consecutive battles in which they proved victorious. October had been a month of defeat for the Confederacy, and while she didn't agree with the Southerners' cause, Adelaide could still sympathize with the loss and feeling of helplessness that was hitting them in waves. She knew the pain of an empty seat at the dinner table.

She was about to turn them in the direction of Elizabeth's house when she felt a shove from behind, sending her through the mouth of an alley and to the ground. She threw her hands out in an attempt to catch herself, but the flesh of her palms scraped against the packed earth as she landed in a heap on the street. A sharp gasp escaped her lips at the pain that burned across her palms, beads of crimson rising to the surface.

Footsteps hurried in behind her as she flipped over and scurried to her feet to find Teo standing between her and Mikaelson. Teo's gun was drawn with his finger poised unflinchingly on the trigger.

"Before you shoot me," Mikaelson said, his hand on the pistol at his hip, "you should know that five men are about to storm into this alley, and they think we're all Union spies. Unless either of you planned on getting shot for treason today, I suggest you run."

Mikaelson bolted through the back door of a shop as a group of men entered the alley. Fear jolted through Adelaide like a bolt of lightning, hot and quick. She grabbed Teo, pulling him with her toward another shop's back door further in the alley. A shot rang out, and she flinched as it embedded itself in the frame of the door she pulled shut behind them. Adelaide shoved a chair under the knob, hoping to buy them a few seconds. Teo rushed to the front door, shaking the handle. He backed up and shoved a shoulder against the door, but it stood firm.

"It won't open," he called to her. "Help me get it loose."

She hurried beside him, and they leaned into it together, but still the door refused to budge. Adelaide banged a fist on it, refusing to accept that this was it. Blood crashed like waves in her ears as she tried to shove her fear to the side. They had to find a way out, but other than the faded walls, she could see no other doors except the one they'd come through and the one they couldn't open. Adelaide snapped her head back to the room as an idea formed in her head. *The walls.*

She ran to the nearest wall and rapped across its length with her knuckles while listening to the sound. Her heart sank with each dense *thunk* that echoed back until halfway along the second wall, she was met with a lighter sound. "Here!" she shouted as the chair holding the knob creaked from the pressure of the men against the door. Adelaide pushed on the wall, releasing the hidden door. "Get in!"

They slipped inside, and Adelaide closed the panel at the sound of wood cracking. The pound of boots shook the floor as she stilled, pressed up against Teo in the darkness. The size of the interior forced her hands to rest on his chest, and she could feel the thrum of his heart beneath her palms. Her own chest rose and fell as she tuned her ears to the men outside. Teo stirred, his movement jostling her. His arm slipped between hers, and he whispered, "Lean back."

She did, and a spark of light ignited between them. In the flame of Teo's lighter, she could see his eyes, nearly black as they blended with the shadows. For what could have been seconds or minutes, they stood like that, still, eyes locked on one another as they waited to be left or found. She wondered how much he could read in her eyes. Unsure of how much of herself she was willing to let them reveal, she dropped her gaze to his chest. Even in the dim light, she could see the faint scrawl of Teo's tattoo through his thin shirt.

"I think they're gone," Teo said, his voice thick.

She let her eyes slide back to his as she listened but only heard silence beyond the wall. Though it was probably safe now, neither of them moved. Teo's eyes flicked to her lips and seemed to ask a question her body was already answering as she leaned in, and he extinguished the flame. Their lips met in the dark as Adelaide gripped Teo's shirt and pulled him toward her. His hands settled on her waist firmly but gently as he pressed her against the wall and deepened the kiss. Her hand trailed along the ink on his chest, and Adelaide suddenly pulled back as the phrase of his tattoo flashed in her mind.

Someday they'll go down together.

"What's wrong?" Teo asked, leaning back, his hands still warm on her hips.

She could feel the lingering presence of his lips on hers and hadn't wanted to break the kiss, but there was only one reason a line from Bonnie Parker's journal would be tattooed over Teo's heart. "Were you in love with Barrow?"

She felt him step back, a cold settling in the space between them. A soft click broke the silence, and light flooded in as Teo released the hidden panel. Adelaide followed him out. He kept his back to her until finally he turned, a weariness in his eyes.

His voice was tight when he spoke. "If you mean Brenna Barrow, then no. Our relationship was complicated to say the least, but romance was never a part of it. Her sister Brynn was the one I loved. I even bought her a ring." A sad laugh escaped his lips. "Hid it in that damn clock Luka won at the auction."

Brynn. It was a name she had only heard once before, from Barrow in the graveyard above the catacombs. "What happened?"

Teo sank into a chair. Resting his elbows on his knees, he laced his fingers on the back of his neck. "Luka ordered a hit on me. I'd been fixing up an old boxing gym for a neighborhood in the suburbs, so he figured the best time to take me out would be when I was there alone. Brynn wanted to see the gym, so I told her to meet me there. I was running late but said she could wait in my office. Luka's cronies had to have been there only minutes before I arrived. Shot right through the frosted glass thinking it was me on the other side."

"I'm so sorry," Adelaide said, a tear slipping down her cheek.

He met her gaze, a sadness and sincerity in their depths that told her his response wasn't just for Brynn. "I am too."

24

CHAPEL HILL

As Adelaide and Teo left the market, shops and storefronts gave way to affluent mansions and sprawling gardens. They were strung together like pearls on a necklace, each modeled in a different era as if their occupants wished for a time other than their own. Adelaide could relate, her mind ever oscillating between looking forward and looking back. The present was a thing she often overlooked, forgetting life was lived in the beautiful between, at least that's what her mother used to say. It seemed no matter how hard she tried, she couldn't get the weight of the past, present, and future to balance evenly. But she was trying.

Adelaide pulled herself from her thoughts as they neared their destination. Her feet slowed to a stop at the base of a small hill. A mansion sat atop it. Light greyish stone made it look as if it were carved from a single rock. The outside was beautiful but plain, the door set back beneath an outcropping of roof supported by six smooth Tuscan pillars. Compared to others on the block, it wasn't the most elaborate dwelling, but what it lacked in architectural detail, it made up for in grandeur. A stone path, lined on either side by a series of flowers and bushes that had somehow remained mostly green despite the impending winter, led to the door.

"Here we are," Adelaide said, her eyes slipping to the large windows overlooking the estate. "Chapel Hill."

"So this is Elizabeth's house?" Teo said as they started down the path.

The hiss of a nearby steam engine pierced the air. "It's the only home she'll ever know. She's never left, except to attend boarding school in the north for a bit when she was younger."

"Guess that explains how a good Southern woman ended up with Union sympathies."

Adelaide nodded. "She's got family up north, too. They were also pretty influential. When her father died and the estate passed to Elizabeth, she set all of their former slaves free. That's actually partly how she grew such an expansive network. Many of her family's former slaves stayed on as paid help or took on other occupations and spied for her."

She could see Teo watching her from the corner of her eye. "Do you think that's why the Red Rose Society wants us to get close to her? Maybe someone in her network knows something they don't?"

Adelaide bit her lip. "Could be." There was no telling what any member of Elizabeth's network could know, let alone Elizabeth, herself. Or what made the information valuable enough to send them back for it. From the suddenness of the first jump, it seemed to Adelaide that Civil War Richmond wasn't originally the intended place for them to travel to. But why change it? "Seems like what we know only scratches the surface of what we don't."

"I'm not surprised." Teo shrugged. "My father operates much the same way. He gives the people under him just enough information for them to feel significant but not enough to shift the balance of power. I've watched him do it for far too long to not notice when someone is playing the long game."

If Adelaide hadn't already been standing still, she would have stopped in her tracks. Teo hardly mentioned his father. In fact, he hardly gave up personal information at all. The fact that he had actually shared about Brynn was something in and of itself. She wondered what had compelled him to trust her with the information, but within a few more steps, they arrived at Elizabeth's door and she lost her opportunity to ask.

Teo lifted the knocker and let it fall back in place. After a few moments of silence, Adelaide could hear the shuffling of footsteps on the other side. The lock clicked and the door slid open. A tall woman answered, her deep brown eyes the color of melted chocolate. "Can I help you folks?"

Adelaide smiled, turning on some Southern charm and hiding her New York accent. The Confederate States in the

1860s was the last place she wanted to sound like a Yankee. "We were wondering if we might have a moment with Ms. Van Lew. Is she home?"

The woman waved them inside to the foyer. "I'll go check with the misses. Who shall I say is calling?"

"Annalise Bordeaux and Mateo Accardi," Adelaide said, realizing they hadn't actually told Elizabeth their names, or their aliases, when they had first met. "Tell her we met last year at the tailor shop over on Elm Street."

The woman left to find Elizabeth, leaving Adelaide and Teo alone in the foyer, the walls papered in pale yellow wildflowers.

"Change it back," Teo said as his eyes swept the room.

"What?"

"Your accent. You didn't use one last time. Elizabeth will get suspicious if you come in sweet talking like a Southern belle." He chuckled, a teasing glint in his eyes. "Plus, it's pretty awful."

Adelaide opened her mouth to refute him, but the woman returned. She clasped her hands gently in front of her. "The misses will see you in the drawing room."

As Adelaide followed behind the woman, the chime of a grandfather clock tolled the hour. She cut her eyes to the sound and met her own reflection in the glass surface of the clock face. Her curls hung loose, heated and pinned in Civil War-style ringlets by Elise before Dr. Jameson had once again swiftly ushered her into the time machine. Her hazel eyes looked like grey storm clouds before the first bolt of lightning lets loose. The image flashed her back to her conversation with Father Jude. As she pulled her eyes from the clock to the walls they passed by, she wondered once again if the girl he had spoken of and the one Kolt was looking for were one and the same. Adelaide knew from Kolt that Sienna had also been having *traces* before she disappeared. If she'd started digging into them like Adelaide had, Sienna could have found her way to Father Jude. But how do you find a girl no one remembers?

They stepped into the drawing room. Sunbeams filtered through the panes of a large window, casting rays of light across the polished wood interior. Elizabeth sat beside a fireplace, unlit logs piled in the grate. Despite the light in the room, she still made her home in the shadows, the dark green of her dress fading into the dark fabric of her chair. She wove a needle and thread along the waistband of a dress and tied the thread off in a knot before handing the dress to the woman who'd led Adelaide and Teo there. An unspoken communication passed between them as the woman gathered the needle and thread and left the room.

"I had a feeling our paths would cross again," Elizabeth said, curiosity alight in her eyes. "Annalise, is it?"

"That's right," Adelaide said, all traces of a Southern accent removed from her words. "What made you think so?"

Elizabeth stood and walked to the window. Light silhouetted her as she gazed sidelong through it to the sprawling estate beyond the glass. "When I was a girl, my parents sent me North for school. There I learned the value of a person lies not in the color of their skin but in the willingness of their heart and capacity to love. That realization lit a fire in me that burned bright, even when I've had to hide the flame." Elizabeth turned from the window, her eyes settling on Adelaide. "I saw that fire in you the first time we met, though I'm still not quite sure what it's burning for. You wear the clothes of an army nurse, but I suspect the war you're fighting is a different one entirely from the one that wages beyond these walls."

Adelaide inhaled, the sharp force of it like a gust of wind in the silent room. What was she fighting for? Her parents? The truth? The life she had, or the one she wanted? She was starting to wonder if any of those things were even worth fighting for at all. Her parents were dead, the truth indistinguishable from the lies and half-truths that concealed it. Even with a time machine, she couldn't go back and she couldn't go forward. So where did that leave her?

Silence stretched on and Elizabeth approached her, cupping Adelaide's hands between her own. Her gaze softened, and Adelaide realized Elizabeth wasn't waiting for an answer. She hadn't even really asked a question. For some reason, Adelaide still felt like she owed her one, but she lacked the words to provide an answer for herself, much less Elizabeth.

Elizabeth released her hands. "Why are you here, dear? And if it's for the same reason as before, my answer remains unchanged."

Adelaide was silent, but her eyes must have betrayed her request.

"I see," Elizabeth said, stepping back and heading to the door. "Eliza will show you out."

Elizabeth was nearly across the threshold when Adelaide's brain caught up with her mouth. "I know about Libby Prison."

Elizabeth stopped, her body rigid as she glanced down either end of the hall and eased back into the room, shutting the door behind her. "And what, exactly, do you think you know about Libby Prison?"

Adelaide knew decidedly more than she could tell Elizabeth, but like with Claire Lacombe back in France, a few well-placed truths might be enough to get Elizabeth to trust her. "Libby got in a new set of Yankee soldiers yesterday. They needed some extra hands for medical care, so I volunteered to help. I overheard a few of the guards talking."

Elizabeth raised an eyebrow. "I can handle a few gossiping guards."

"They were talking about you." Adelaide gripped her skirt in her hands and closed the gap between her and Elizabeth, laying all of her cards on the table. "You and I both know you bring more than casseroles and minor comforts in and out of that prison. And the guards are starting to suspect so, too. They think you're hiding contraband in the bottom of your casserole warmer."

The guards were right. Though Elizabeth never left Richmond, she was an active participant in her own spy ring. For months now she had been bringing coded messages, contraband and even prisoners in and out of Libby Prison. She'd even made a secret room in her house to hide Union escapees before she could funnel them safely out of the city. In a few years, she would help orchestrate a massive prison break from Libby. If she was caught before the war ended, it would be a massive blow to the Union, one so large it could mean a Confederate victory. And for Elizabeth, it could mean her head.

Elizabeth propped her chin on her fist. She opened her mouth to speak, but as she did, the door to the drawing room burst open.

"Elizabeth—" the man said, his words cutting short at the realization she wasn't alone. "I'm sorry to interrupt, but I'm afraid I must speak with you. Now."

Something in the man's mannerisms must have alerted her to the seriousness of the problem. Without so much as a glance back, she followed him out, leaving the door to bang into place behind them.

"Would you say that was more or less successful than our last attempt?" Teo asked as he spun the orb of an antique globe around its axis. The faded colors of the continents ran together in a blur.

Adelaide blew out a breath. She wondered if this, too, was a losing battle. Why wouldn't Elizabeth trust her? And why did the Red Rose Society care if she did? "I guess we'll just see ourselves out."

They left the drawing room and turned left, following the path back to the front door. As Adelaide's hand hit the knob and eased it open, a voice called behind her. "Annalise!"

Adelaide turned, the door knob slipping from her grip as Elizabeth raced toward her, skirt bunched in her hands. She skidded to a stop in front of Adelaide, and her cheeks flushed from the effort. Her eyes held hesitation, but she spoke anyway, her words crisp and clear. "If you're still willing to offer it, I could use your help."

25

STITCHED IN SECRETS

OCTOBER 23, 1862
RICHMOND, VIRGINIA

Turns out the Confederate White House was fairly easy to get into. All Adelaide had to do was walk through the back door. She carried a fresh bouquet of hydrangeas and a secret, stitched into the waistband of her dress. The garment was not her own, but the pale grey-blue of the one Elizabeth had been darning when Adelaide and Teo walked into the drawing room.

At this point in the war, Elizabeth's ring had gotten into a rhythm. Each member knew their part and played it to perfection, but even so, things didn't always go according to plan. Instead of words, Elizabeth's ring spoke in symbols stitched in quilts, ciphers scrawled on paper and pinpricks struck through book pages, so when she saw a red shirt hanging from the clothesline outside the White House on her walk that morning, she knew a covert message was waiting for her at the seamstress.

One of Elizabeth's former slaves, Mary Jane Bowser, was stationed right in the heart of the Confederate White House. When Elizabeth freed her, the bond they shared as girls became a partnership in espionage as women. Now, Mary Jane was on the inside as the personal slave to the Southern states' First Lady. Mary Jane was perhaps one of the Union's greatest assets. Not only did she have access to the man who ran the war against them, she had access to his study and the correspondence that passed through his fingertips, along with an eidetic memory to recall exactly what they said from only a glance.

According to Elizabeth, all Adelaide had to do was bring the flowers to Mary Jane and retrieve the message she had for Elizabeth. She was already expecting the flowers as Jefferson Davis had placed an order for his wife. The brooch at her neck with a clover attached to it would tell Mary Jane she could pass along the message. Adelaide should be in and out in no time. Or so she hoped.

She thrust her shoulders back and held her head high, trying to convince herself and those she passed that she belonged there. At the end of the main corridor, the hall split off in three directions. Adelaide hesitated, trying to remember what Elizabeth had said about navigating the interior of the White House, but she couldn't recall anything about the three offshoots. Had she missed a turn? She doubled back and found the right path, marked as Elizabeth said it would be by a grand piano in the center hall. Passing the piano, she took the corridor behind it.

As she followed the path, Adelaide could hear the strong baritone of a man's voice in the hall she had just come from. It edged closer, working its way toward her. Her heart raced as she slipped into a room. She eased the door slowly shut behind her and rested her back against the cool wood. The room was empty and recently polished with a light hint of fresh lemon perfuming the air. Dark wood glistened in the afternoon light, falling on the large desk in front of the window—a desk that could only belong to Jefferson Davis. She'd found his office.

Adelaide only intended to wait for the footsteps to pass, but as she took in the room a new idea began to form. When Elizabeth stopped her at the door, she'd told Adelaide this was a onetime thing, but the fact that she'd even asked for Adelaide's help had to mean something. If she provided some information of her own, maybe it would be enough to get her into Elizabeth's good graces.

As she approached the desk, a pain sparked at her brow. Wincing, she came to stand behind it. As tidy as the room was, so was Jefferson Davis' desk. Books were stacked in neat piles, a series of pens aligned just so and a carving of a bird sat atop a bundle of opened letters like a paperweight. She flipped through them, the flicker of images passing through her mind as the paper grazed her skin, but Adelaide knew she didn't have time to sift through them and discern their meaning.

She had to act fast. Teo had been less than thrilled about the idea of her walking into the Confederate White House alone, but Elizabeth had convinced him it was safer that way. Still, she figured she had about twenty more minutes before Teo came looking for her. The last thing she needed was for him to barge into the White House and get them arrested for espionage.

Most of the letters were in code—from the interior message down to who had sent them. Adelaide wished she could bring them with her, but she had no place to hide them, and besides, if she took them, Jefferson Davis would know he had a mole. Finally, she found a message that was partially decoded. Someone, probably Jefferson, had underlined every fifth word and transcribed the letters beneath so that the message read: *The target is a nurse.* The message in and of itself was alarming, not in the least because Adelaide had come back to Richmond this time as a Civil War nurse, but the name decoded beneath it shocked her even more: *Rathbone.* Adelaide slipped the letter out, trying to read more of the message that had yet to be decoded, but as her eyes set on the paper, the door to the office opened.

A woman walked in, her dark skin gleaming like the polished desktop. She froze when she spotted Adelaide. Her eyes shifted from the letters to the flowers and back to Adelaide's face. "Who are you? What are you doing in here?"

"I'm Lucy," Adelaide said, placing the letters back and picking up the hydrangeas. "I have a flower delivery for Mrs. Davis. I, ah, got a little turned around. I'm supposed to give them to Mary Jane." Adelaide knew she was rambling, but the letter had sparked something in her mind—a memory of the day her Red Rose Society letter arrived and the book on the Civil War she had been reading before it came. She could have sworn the words changed on the page, revealing a foreign history in which Rathbone had been a Confederate spy and not just a Union officer.

"Let's go," the woman said, coming up beside Adelaide. "You shouldn't be in here—" Her eyes found the clover, carved in the soft white flesh of a peach pit and understanding lit on her features as her voice dropped to a whisper. "I'm Mary Jane. Why did Elizabeth send you?"

Footsteps echoed in the hall, their quickened pace bringing with them the voices of two men arguing. Adelaide's pulse raced as they stopped outside the office.

"Grab the flowers," Mary Jane said, straightening the bird carving. "Quick."

Adelaide didn't need to be told twice. She swiped the bouquet from the desk and followed Mary Jane, who tapped a panel on the wall and pushed Adelaide inside. She followed behind her and shut the passage just as the main door opened with a bang on the other side. Darkness swallowed them whole, but Adelaide could just make out Mary Jane, a finger to her lips as she pressed her ear against the wall. Adelaide did the same.

"I need more men, Jefferson. It's as simple as that. You know as well as I do that war is a numbers game and right now, we're at least sixty-thousand short. We've got more men deserting every day than we do taking on the fight. If things keep up at the rate they're going, our army will completely melt away by Christmas and we'll be ringing in the New Year under Lincoln again."

"What do you want me to do, Robert? I can't summon men from thin air. Maybe if you started winning more battles it would be Yankee blood soaking the ground and their men losing morale."

"I want you to do whatever it takes to convince those deserting to stay and those not fighting to join. My men and I are fighting the war from out there. We need you to do your part in here."

The conversation went on like that for several more minutes before Mary Jane stopped listening and motioned for Adelaide to follow her. When they were a ways from the office, Mary Jane stopped and turned to her. "Why did Elizabeth send you?"

"The seamstress, she had to meet the train to receive her brother's remains."

Mary Jane shook her head. "This war has robbed far too many men of a life they have barely even begun to live. I knew Peter. He was just a boy. I suppose Louisa will be the one making the arrangements. They were all each other had left."

"I'm sorry."

"I'll have to find a way to get that dress with the message back so I can burn it before Louisa's replacement finds it. I already dropped it off for her to give to Elizabeth." She continued down the passage. "Come on, I'll code a new letter for you and swap it out with the one you're carrying. Elizabeth needs this information. Now."

26

MATCHES TO MATCHES

———

"Hey you," Adelaide said, not sure what to expect as she stepped into Xander's studio. He had wanted to talk after the auction, but another impromptu trip to the past had taken precedence, and after playing spy for a day, all Adelaide had wanted to do when she got back was sleep. She did, for a while, until her dreams filled with a mix of memories from Richmond and her days at the diner when she'd been reading on break and watched the words change on the pages of her book.

Xander sat back against a wall, his legs extended before him and eyes glazed from sleep. "Hey, you. What are you doing here?"

Adelaide dropped to the ground beside him and leaned back. "Couldn't sleep. I thought maybe if you were up, we could talk. Always seemed to help me before."

Xander tilted his head and rubbed the back of his neck. "Actually, there's something I wanted to give you."

"Give me? Why?"

He stood and held his hands out, helping her to her feet before walking toward a covered canvas in the center of the room. He grabbed the edge of the sheet and tugged, revealing the finished painting of the lighthouse.

Adelaide gasped. "Xander, it's beautiful."

And it was. Jeweled tones of sapphire and emerald now mixed in the waves, tossed against the outcropping of rocks by the incoming tide. What had started as a daytime scene had morphed into an evening one, depicting the moments right before the sun slipped beneath the horizon, washing the world in a golden haze.

Xander shoved his hands in his pockets. "I started this painting in Europe last summer. Got about halfway through it when I realized I couldn't finish it. Not because I didn't know what it needed to be but because it made me think of you, and I wasn't quite ready to process the thought that I might never see you again."

"Xander—" Adelaide began.

"Wait, please. Let me finish."

Adelaide nodded, not trusting herself to speak.

"Do you remember what you said that night we spent stargazing on the beach?"

She said a lot of things that night beneath the stars, but only one of them could have led Xander to capture the scene in paint. "I want to freeze this moment in time and live in it for eternity."

Xander smiled, but it didn't quite reach his eyes. "When you showed up in my life again and I picked the painting back up, I thought I was finishing it for me, to help me process the last year. And although that was part of it, I realized I was really painting it for you. I've never seen you as free and happy as you were that night. I hoped that maybe by having a piece of that place you'd be able to find some of that peace and happiness again. Maybe we both could."

Tears welled in the corners of her eyes as she reached for Xander's hand, twining it with her own. Words couldn't describe how desperately she wanted to find that girl again, to finally feel like she could breathe and believe there was more to life than pain and more to her than the scars she carried. "Thank you, truly."

Xander smiled again. This time it reached his eyes as he sensed, like she did, the final cracks in their friendship beginning to heal. He nudged her shoulder with his, "You're welcome."

A crash sounded in the main room. Adelaide jumped, releasing her grip on Xander's hand as Charlie came running into the studio. "There you two are. I've been looking for you everywhere. I finally had to ping your phones."

"Isn't that illegal?" Adelaide said.

"Yeah, well so is being a murderer," Charlie said, her eyes glinting. "And I think I just found ours."

"What do you mean?" Xander said. "I thought you ran the print already and came up empty."

"I did, but I've been cycling it through different databases, and I finally got a match." Charlie bit her lip and scrunched her face. "It's nearly identical to a print the police pulled from the break-in at Holyrood."

"A match to who?" Adelaide said, unsure if after all this time she truly wanted to know the answer.

"There's no picture, but there is a name." Charlie turned her laptop around so they could see the screen.

An enlarged picture of the print filled the left side. A second print was superimposed over it with a series of green dots alight on all the major whorls and dips that aligned between the two. On the right, was an empty rectangle where a photograph would normally be and below it, a single name in big black letters: **Léon, Pauline**.

Adelaide knocked on the door to Kolt's apartment, breathing in the mix of coffee and maple from where the scents below melded with the ones above. After knocking a second time, the door slid slowly open. Kolt blinked against the light, his eyes finally focusing on Adelaide standing before him.

"You know, it's perfectly acceptable to visit a friend during the day." Kolt's voice slurred with sleep. "But if you insist on continuing to visit me in the wee hours of the night, let me know so I can just give you a key." He smirked, clearly amused with his joke, but it didn't last long, wiped clean from his face like chalk from a board the moment his eyes took in Xander and Charlie behind her. "What's going on?"

Adelaide shook her head. "Not here. Can we come in?"

Kolt stepped to the side, holding the door for them as they entered. Charlie and Xander sat at the island while Kolt leaned against it on the other side, unintentionally mirroring Xander. Black and blond, the two were like night and day. Adelaide paced between them, her feet following a natural groove in the worn floorboards as she shared her story, starting with the fire and ending with the DNA match to Pauline.

"Let me get this straight," Kolt said, his eyes tracking her pacing. "The DNA the police pulled from the fire and the DNA left behind on another modern-day crime scene is the same DNA. And, the match is a girl you met hundreds of years in the past when you jumped to the French Revolution during initiation. Did I miss anything."

"That about covers it," Adelaide forced herself to stop pacing and braced her hands on the counter. "Except for the fact that someone tried to cover up that she was there the night of the fire, and if it's for the reason we think it is, she might have started it."

Adelaide couldn't make sense of it all, but she'd followed the clues and somehow, they'd led her to Pauline.

"So what do we do now?" Charlie asked, her fingers working at a curl.

Silence followed until Adelaide's voice worked its way up her throat and broke it. "We find her."

"But how?" Charlie asked, her hazel eyes alight with the curiosity of a mystery.

Adelaide had been waiting for that question. She knew its answer wouldn't be easy and it could jeopardize the future each of them had joined the Red Rose Society to build. It was also the reason she had wanted to come to Kolt's. They were going to need a pilot. "We take the time machine."

"Impossible," Xander said, his fingers twitching at his side. "Believe me. I want to find this girl as much as you do, but there's no way we're getting that machine. They keep it under constant surveillance and even if we could get our hands on it, it's too dangerous to go back to France. I'm sorry, but it's not worth the risk."

"We wouldn't have to go back to France," Adelaide said.

"What do you mean?" Kolt asked, a brow raised. "I thought you said she was in Paris?"

Adelaide hesitated, but as the face of a girl crossed her mind in a memory, she knew the truth of what she'd seen that day. "I saw her, Pauline. In the market the first time we jumped to Richmond. And I'm pretty sure she saw me too. I have a plan, but I need each of you to pull it off. Do you trust me?"

Adelaide lay in bed watching the clock slip slowly from one hour to the next. After going through the plan in her head for the fifteenth time, the red numbers on the clock finally marked the hour she'd been waiting for. She eased out of bed, slipping across the floor and out the door as she listened to the steady rise and fall of Elise's breath fade behind her. Her heart raced, her own breath sounding far too loud in her ears as she pushed the button on the elevator door for the sublevel.

She felt bad leaving Elise behind, but there would be no changes to history for her to track until Adelaide and the others came back from Richmond. She knew Elise would kill her when she found out, but Adelaide would deal with it when the time came. Until then, she had made Charlie promise to fill Elise in when she woke up.

The doors opened and Adelaide half expected to be stopped by guards as she crossed the catwalk and descended the stairs to the apparatus floor, but she was the only one there. She eyed the video cameras around the room, her hand moving to the coms unit in her ear. "Charlie? Can you see me?"

Static crackled in her ear before Charlie's voice came through on the other end. "You're a ghost, my friend. I looped the feed, so as far as anyone can tell, the place is empty."

"Perfect, now hurry down here." Adelaide said, her nerves a heavy brick in the base of her stomach. "I want to get there and back before anyone notices we're gone."

"Got it," Charlie said, the com going silent.

The elevator dinged again and both Kolt and Xander got out, their quickened pace suggesting they couldn't leave each other's company fast enough. She wondered if they'd talked at all on the ride down and if so, what it had been about.

"Ready for this?" Kolt asked as they descended the steps.

"Yeah, it'll be fine," Adelaide said, not sure who she was trying to reassure more, Kolt or herself. As much as she craved the truth, the thought of finally getting it equally thrilled and terrified her. She wasn't sure which emotion was stronger, but after so long she finally had a lead and the risk of not taking it scared her more than the risk of jumping in.

They quickly changed clothes and returned to the apparatus floor to find Charlie. She glanced up at them as her fingers continued flying across a keyboard. "Have everything you need?"

Adelaide did a once-over at her outfit ready to confirm they were all set, but another voice spoke before she had the chance.

"Not yet you don't." Teo stepped down off the final step, fully dressed as he had been the last few times they'd gone to Richmond. "And before you even think about coming up with a lie to tell me about why all of you are here right now, you should probably know I followed you the other night and heard everything, so you can either let me come with you or I'll go wake Matriarch up right now and tell her what you're up to."

"I'm sure my grandmother would love that," Kolt said, crossing his arms. "But either way, we don't have time to debate it."

Teo walked the final few paces to Adelaide, his gaze steady on hers. "What's it gonna be?"

"Fine," Adelaide said. There was no point in arguing with him. "You can come."

"Sorry, Xander," Kolt said, pushing the panel on the side of the time machine. "You're out. We can only safely take three people."

"Yeah," Xander scoffed, not bothering to hide his disdain. "I knew I was out the moment Teo showed up."

Adelaide threw Xander a sympathetic look, but he had already rounded the console and taken a seat beside Charlie.

"Alright, you three," Charlie checked the monitor. "I ran an algorithm I've been working on to track people in time. It's still in its early phase, but Pauline should be somewhere near Richmond and the date it wants to drop you in is May 31, 1864. You've got about a day's worth of time after you land to find her and get back. Good luck."

27

SPIES AND ASHES

MAY 31, 1864
RICHMOND, VIRGINIA

Moisture hung thick in the air, soaking the fabric of Adelaide's dress and coating her skin in a fine layer of mist. It was unbearably hot for May, making the weather all the more intolerable. She panted, out of breath despite having traveled the road between the grove and the market twice before. The low bun she had corralled her hair into was already expanding, a few loose curls sticking to her temples.

Adelaide took a breath, almost choking on the acrid air. Charcoal and tar hung in the atmosphere so thick she could taste the burn of it on her tongue. Memories of the fire flickered in her head, calling her back to the last time she'd forced such air into her lungs.

"What is that smell?" Teo coughed, his eyes watering.

Ash drifted on the lazy breeze, no more cooling than a warm breath. "They're burning bodies."

Leaving the fields behind, they entered the market, an outright ghost town compared to the last few times they had passed through it. Barrels of tar sat on every corner. They licked flames and heat into the sky as each attempted to wick away the foul odor that plagued the streets of Richmond. A handful of patrons wandered the stalls half-heartedly as they dabbed their brows with handkerchiefs or held them over their mouths. Only a few vendors had set up for the day, but luckily, one was selling what Adelaide was looking for.

"I'd like these items please, sir," Adelaide pointed out a fountain pen, inkwell and a small piece of parchment to the merchant.

He tallied up the price and she handed over the money while he wrapped the goods in paper and tied them with twine. "Good day, miss." He bowed his head.

Adelaide thanked the man and wished him the same, hoping he hadn't noticed the way her hands trembled as she took the package. She gripped the wrapping and tried to steady herself as she let the possibilities of the next few hours wash over her.

Truth be told, she wasn't sure what she was feeling. In the time since her parents died, she'd run the gamut of emotions, seeming to feel everything and nothing all at once. In newspaper clippings and the ruins of her childhood home, Adelaide had been looking for answers since the last ember from the fire cooled, but never once had she thought Pauline may be the one to provide them. It shouldn't be possible for a girl from the French Revolution to be in Civil War Richmond, let alone Adelaide's house or Holyrood Palace. But then again, Adelaide had spent the past few months walking streets and times that were not her own.

She checked to see if she was being followed before ducking into the alley Mikaelson had pushed her into on their last trip. When she was sure no one was watching, she slipped into the abandoned shop. Adelaide paused at the threshold and ran her fingers over the bullet lodged in the door frame. She swallowed, aware of the danger they were in, and while it wasn't the Red Rose Society holding a time limit over their heads, the clock was still ticking.

Inside, the shop was much the same. Wallpaper had begun to peel, revealing discolored beams of wood beneath. The chair she'd jammed the door with lay in splintered pieces on the floor. Kolt stood near the opposite door, gazing through the dusty windows as Teo leaned against the adjacent wall, directly in front of the hidden panel. Their eyes connected, a blush rising to her cheeks as she recalled the feel of his hands on her and the press of his lips against her own. He seemed to know what she was thinking as the corner of his mouth raised ever so slightly. Adelaide averted her gaze and approached the worn counter. She placed the bundle on top and began removing its contents.

"Why are we writing a letter to Elizabeth when we can just go knock on her door?" Teo said. Having made his way to the counter, he now stood behind her, his gaze cast over her shoulder to the items in her hands.

"Because," Adelaide said, removing the stopper from the ink vial and dipping the pen in its center, "we don't know if she's there, and even if she is, she's being watched. A few months ago on this timeline, she initiated a prison break from Libby Prison. She won't be charged because no one is able to provide proof, but their suspicions are enough. They aren't going to let her pull a stunt like that again any time soon. It's too dangerous for us to go to her house."

Adelaide finished up the letter and set the pen aside. Removing her dagger, she poised the needle-like blade carefully above the parchment. She still had one thing left to do before she sealed it.

If anyone opened the letter, they would find a piece of friendly correspondence, inquiring about Elizabeth's well-being and her mother's health. But when Elizabeth looked closer, as she was sure to do with every letter that passed through her fingers, she'd find the smallest of punctures in the parchment below the letters that spelled out the real message. Adelaide picked up the pen once more and scrawled *Annalise* at the bottom of the letter before folding it up and tying it tightly with the twine from the package.

They exited the storefront and headed back out into the market. A young newsboy stood on the outskirts and fanned himself with a fistful of periodicals. He perked up a bit as she approached.

"How much for the rest of the papers?" Adelaide asked.

He blinked slowly. "You want 'em all, miss?"

She nodded. "I'll pay you double the cost if you deliver this letter to Elizabeth Van Lew for me. Do you know who she is?"

He eyed her, his eyes widening as he took in the money in her hand. "Aye, miss. I can find her."

Adelaide handed the boy the letter and the coins. "Tell Elizabeth she can find us at the Ballard Hotel."

He pocketed both and slipped out of sight.

"How do we know he'll actually deliver it?" Kolt asked, watching the boy disappear around the corner.

She watched him too, knowing the direction he headed was opposite of Chapel Hill. "We don't,"

The Ballard Hotel sat on the intersection of Franklin and Fourteenth. It consisted of two buildings, one each in Greek and Italian style that somehow managed to both complement and juxtapose one another. A covered, cast-iron bridge, forged from the same metal that in recent years had made travel and shipment by steam engine possible, connected the two. As one of the most prestigious hotels in Richmond, the Ballard had played host to the likes of Dickens and Poe. Artists and politicians still graced its halls, but in the years since the war began, spies on both sides had found themselves guests at the hotel or visitors to the shops housed on the main floor.

Though it was day, fog and ash covered Richmond in a veil of dark that blurred the edges of the city like an old photograph. Their boots sounded on the bridge as they crossed from one side to the other. Hoping to spot Elizabeth, Adelaide cast her gaze through the arched windows to the street below. She knew it had been a risk using the boy to run the letter. It was a longshot asking Elizabeth for information on Pauline, but if the girl was anywhere in Richmond, Elizabeth would know about it.

They followed the bellhop to a room on the third floor. Adelaide unlocked the door, greeted inside by plum-colored wallpaper and plush carpet. A plated mirror reflected the single bed across from it, and a wooden writing desk sat beside the only window. Teo crossed the room and dropped onto the bed. Pulling out his lighter, he lit the taper on the nightstand. Snapping it shut, he proceeded to flick it open and closed in a steady rhythm like the ticking of a clock.

Kolt offered Adelaide the chair at the desk, but she shook her head, content to let her feet wander so her mind wouldn't. He sat, turning the chair to face her as she paced at the foot of the bed. "What did you write to Elizabeth? In the coded message, I mean?"

Teo sat up straighter against the headboard, his eyes curious.

"I told her we started working as spies for Allan Pinkerton, a detective and spy for the Union. I said we'd been tracking a potential Confederate spy by the name of Pauline Léon and that we lost track of her around the Richmond area. Wanted to inquire if Elizabeth had heard anything about her."

"Do you think she'll come?" Teo asked, still fidgeting with his lighter. "We haven't exactly had the best luck when it comes to Van Lew."

Adelaide bit her lip, eyes narrowed. "I can't be sure, but I think she will. It's a big enough risk to the Union that she might feel it's worth pursuing."

"Let's hope you're right." Kolt ran his hands over the starch fabric of his pants. "What do we know about Pauline anyway?"

"Not much," Adelaide caught sight of herself in the mirror. She pulled her hair loose and began working it back into a bun at the base of her neck. Teo's eyes met hers in the reflection as each of their thoughts turned to their time in Paris. "She founded the Society of Revolutionary Republican Women with Claire Lacombe during the French Revolution, but after that, I'm not sure. History lost track of her."

Kolt leaned back in his chair, mulling over her words. "Can we trust her?"

A knock sounded at the door. All three of their heads whipped to the sound. Teo eased off the bed and padded softly to the door. "Who is it?"

"Well, it's not the maid."

Teo looked to Adelaide.

She nodded, confirming she, too, recognized Elizabeth's voice. "Let her in."

Teo opened the door, and Elizabeth entered in a flurry of dark skirts. She nodded a greeting to Adelaide before stopping short as she spotted Kolt. "Who is this?"

"This is Will." Adelaide said, gesturing to Kolt and hoping his presence didn't prevent Elizabeth from telling them what she'd discovered. "He's been helping us track Pauline."

Kolt inclined his head. "Ms. Van Lew."

Elizabeth lingered on him a moment more before returning the recognition and turning back to Adelaide. "Are you sure the Pauline you are looking for is near Richmond?"

"Yes," Adelaide dared to hope Elizabeth brought good news. "We're certain she's in the city or the surrounding area."

Elizabeth frowned, her eyes darkening. "I've heard rumors of a young woman. She's been reported at several Union camps as a nurse, has even taken care of men at the bloodiest battles this war has shown so far, but when the bullets stop, she disappears. No one knows her name, but our soldiers have come to call her Pauline of the Potomac."

Words from the decoded message she'd seen on Jefferson Davis' desk flashed in Adelaide's mind. *The target is a nurse.* What if the message wasn't referring to her but to Pauline?

But even so, why would Rathbone be looking for Pauline? "It has to be her." Adelaide wondered what it all meant. "Do you know where she is now?"

"She's tending soldiers at a Union encampment outside Mechanicsville, about twelve miles from here. I've already arranged for my stablehand to meet you in front of the post office with some horses. I must be going before my tails get suspicious. The rest is up to you."

28

COLD HARBOR

MAY 31, 1864
RICHMOND, VIRGINIA

True to her word, Elizabeth's stablehand was waiting for them in front of the post office. In each hand he gripped the reigns of a dark stallion, their coats the rainbow-black color of spilled ink. The larger horse whinnied and tossed his head in a majestic arc as they approached.

Teo eyed the creatures warily. "Are you sure we can't just take the train? I hear travel by steam engine is all the rage these days."

"Have you never ridden a horse before?" Adelaide was genuinely surprised.

"I prefer transport that can't think for itself."

Adelaide took the reins from the stable hand and passed one to Kolt. Turning back to Teo she added, "Who would you rather ride with?"

He looked between the two horses. "Depends. Who's more likely to get me there in one piece?"

Kolt tightened his horse's girth and led it alongside them. "That would be Adelaide."

She placed her foot in the stirrup and swung up onto the horse. After shifting her weight in the saddle, she held a hand out to Teo. He took it, mimicking her earlier motions as he settled in place behind her and circled his arms around her waist.

"This here's Blackjack," the stablehand said, stroking the muzzle of Kolt's horse. "And this one's Apollo. He's got a map in his saddle bag if ya need it. Once you get outta the city, Mechanicsville's a straight shot northeast."

Adelaide thanked the man and clicked her tongue as she squeezed her legs against the horse's side. Teo's grip tightened as Apollo shifted into a walk. They followed the map out of Richmond, letting the horses' muscles warm before coaxing them to a trot at the edge of the city.

Farms and fields flew by, giving way to forest. As the war progressed, more and more lumber was needed for fortifications and fires, leaving a series of stump-ridden clearings between patches of trees. They rode for several miles before Adelaide slowed them to a stop at a split in the road. She looked either which way, unsure which path was the correct one to take. "Hand me the map."

She reached a hand behind her to Teo, who placed it in her palm, and proceeded to unfold the parchment. Adelaide startled as something fell on her lap, tumbling from the folds.

"What is that?" Kolt peered over from his seat on Blackjack.

Adelaide picked up the item, her eyes widening as she read the words scrawled on its face. "It's a letter, addressed to General Grant."

"*The* General Grant?" Kolt asked.

"I doubt there're two Union generals at this time who go by that name," Teo said. "What should we do with it?"

Adelaide wasn't sure. If they were stopped by Confederates, carrying such a letter could condemn them to death. Was Elizabeth expecting them to deliver it or was there another reason it was in their saddle bag? "I don't know, but until we make a decision, I'm not risking putting it back in the bag." She tucked it into the waistband of her skirt for safe keeping.

They followed the path to the right, forcing the horses into a gallop that only slowed to a walk a few times to give the stallions a break before they reached the outskirts of a camp. White tents, pitched in staggered rows like Gideon's chess board, filled the clearing. Smoke spilled from campfires interspersed among the tents and filled the air with an aroma quickly choked out by that from the larger fires burning in the distance. A group of soldiers, muskets gripped between their palms, met them about a mile out as they approached. Sweat formed on Adelaide's brow. Her nerves eased only when she took in the dark blue of their uniforms, signifying they were Union soldiers.

"Afternoon, ma'am." The soldier in the lead tipped his hat to Adelaide before casting a suspicious eye on Teo and Kolt. "Gentlemen. Can I be of service?"

Adelaide sat up straighter, letting an easy smile settle on her lips. "Afternoon, soldier. We were actually the ones hoping to be of service today. We've just come from Richmond with a correspondence for the general."

The soldier eased a bit but remained firmly planted between them and the camp. "Might I ask who the letter is from?"

Adelaide hesitated, hoping she was right about what Elizabeth had wanted her to do with the it. "Elizabeth Van Lew."

A beat passed before the soldier nodded. "Very well. Robertson." He addressed a thin man behind him. "See these three to the general, and when they have delivered their correspondence, see them out."

"Yes, sir," the soldier said. Palm forward at his temple, he gave a salute and motioned for them to follow him.

The other soldiers moved to either side of the road, clearing a path. Adelaide released the breath she had been holding, grateful to have gotten this far, but well aware the hurdles between her and the truth were far from over.

"You can leave your horses here," the soldier said. He held a hand out to Adelaide, and she handed him the reins, which he proceeded to tie to a nearby post. Once secure, he returned his hand to her, waiting expectantly to help her down off the horse.

Adelaide was perfectly capable of dismounting a horse on her own, but she also wasn't about to snub an act of chivalry. She took his hand and swung her leg off the saddle, her feet hitting the soft earth beside the man. "Thank you, sir."

Teo vaulted from the horse as Kolt dismounted his own and tied Blackjack's reins beside Apollo's.

They followed the soldier through the camp and passed several of his brothers-in-arms along the way. Some sat beside the fire and scraped the bottoms of their bowls so as to not waste a crumb of their meager rations. Others stood in groups, smoking and conversing with one another. But all held in their eyes both a weariness that said they could not withstand another day of war and a determination that said they would see their cause to the end. Adelaide knew enough about the Civil War to know only half the men she set eyes on today would still be breathing by the time it ended a year from now. And of those who did survive, many would be crippled or mentally scarred from all they'd seen and done in the name of country.

At last, they approached the opening of a tent. The soldier left them at the threshold and instructed them to wait while he informed the general of their arrival.

"Have you seen her yet?" Adelaide whispered to Teo. She swept her eyes around the camp as she had while they walked, but Pauline was nowhere in sight.

Teo shook his head and Adelaide tried not to show the disappointment on her face as the soldier leaned through the opening and swept the flap aside for them to enter. Inside, the tent was sparse, but neat. A cot covered the ground on the right, a small trunk positioned beside it and topped with a lantern. Across the way from the cot stood a wooden table with maps sprawled across its surface. The only other furniture in the tent was a desk along the back wall. Grant sat behind it and peered up at them as they entered. He closed the book he had been writing in and stood.

For a man who commanded the Union army and had such a presence on paper, Grant, himself looked perfectly ordinary. He was short and thin with mouse-brown hair and a beard. The dark grey of his eyes collected like storm clouds, but they held a kindness and curiosity as he watched them. "Thank you, Robertson. That will be all," he said, dismissing the soldier.

"It's an honor to meet you, sir," Adelaide bowed her head to him.

"The honor is all mine, my dear." Grant returned the bow. "To what do I owe the pleasure."

Adelaide retrieved the letter from her waistband and handed it to him. "We have a message for you from Elizabeth Van Lew."

Grant popped the wax seal and ran his eyes along the message. The crease in his brow deepened as he read. "Impossible, I—"

"General!" A soldier ran into the tent as a shot resounded nearby. "Confederates have breached the east woods and are advancing toward camp."

Grant's face darkened as he retrieved his gun and held the letter to the flame of his lamp. The corner ignited, spreading up the parchment until it consumed Elizabeth's words. "Tell the men to head them off on the southern flank."

The soldier left and Grant returned his gaze to Adelaide. "I trust you can see yourselves out to safety," he said, belting his saber and slipping through the folds of the tent.

Adelaide, with Teo and Kolt on her heels, ran out behind Grant into a world erupted in chaos. Hues of dark blue streaked across her vision as soldiers dropped their bowls and cigarettes to pick up weapons and run toward the eastern woods at the edge of the camp. Guns continued to crack like fireworks, cutting through men on both sides as a sea of grey soldiers emerged from the trees. The haunting cries of wounded men pierced the air like a siren call to death.

"That's it." Teo grabbed Adelaide's wrist as he led her back toward the horses. "We're leaving."

"No." Adelaide wrenched her arm from his grip. "We can't leave yet."

"Ad," Kolt said, trying to reason with her. "I know you want to find Pauline, but other than a rumor, we have no proof she's here. Answers aren't worth the price of your life."

"She's here." Adelaide jutted out her jaw. She knew she was being stubborn and rash, but she didn't care. This might be her only chance to finally learn the truth. "You heard what Elizabeth said. Pauline shows up at the bloodiest battles and helps tend the wounded soldiers. Well, this is the Battle of Cold Harbor and one of the worst ones of the war."

"We don't have time for this," Teo argued back with her as the fighting grew louder. Adelaide knew there was no convincing him otherwise. He'd sooner throw her over his shoulder and tie her to the saddle than risk any of them catching a stray bullet as the battle intensified. She knew he was right, but she wasn't about to give him the opportunity. One way or another, she wasn't leaving without answers.

"I have to know." She grabbed her skirts and darted into the melee.

"Adelaide!" Teo called behind her, but she was already lost in the crowd.

29

TIES THAT BIND

———

MAY 31, 1864
RICHMOND, VIRGINIA

Adelaide wove in and out of the rows of tents. Soldiers jostled her on all sides as they filtered the opposite direction. It wasn't until a flash of grey caught her eye that she realized she wasn't the only one moving against the tide. In the same moment, the woman turned, and Adelaide recognized once again the face she had seen in the market that first day in Richmond. *Pauline.*

Pauline whipped around, picking up her pace as she slipped into the next row. Adelaide followed suit, tracking the girl like a bloodhound. To her surprise, Pauline didn't try to shake her, almost as if she was running to something instead of away. Without a moment's hesitation, Pauline ran straight through the flap of a nearby tent. After a few more paces, Adelaide, too, slipped inside.

Pauline stood hunched over a trunk and rifled through its contents. "You just couldn't leave it alone. Could you?"

Pauline was still talking, her back to Adelaide, but she didn't hear any of it. White hot anger flared inside her like a kettle about to boil over. She was angry at her parents for dying, Charlie for lying, Xander for leaving and herself for not being able to move past it all. Before Adelaide knew it, she was lunging at Pauline. The two of them fell to the floor, rolling over one another as they each fought for the advantage. Despite her small stature, Pauline was surprisingly strong. She managed to place several solid blows before Adelaide pinned her on her back and pressed a dagger to her neck.

Pauline stilled, and Adelaide watched as the artery in the girl's neck pulsed beneath her blade. She increased the pressure ever so slightly and Pauline inhaled sharply as the dagger bit into her neck, drawing beads of crimson to the surface.

Pauline cut her eyes at Adelaide. "Do it and you'll never know what really happened that night."

Adelaide flinched but held the dagger in place. "What do you know about it?"

A sly smile crawled up Pauline's face. She might be the one with a dagger at her throat, but Pauline had the upper hand, and they both knew it. "I'll tell you what you want to know, but first we have to find your mother's journal before Rathbone gets back."

Adelaide jerked, taken aback by the mention of Rathbone and her mother's missing journal. "Her journal is here? How?"

"Rathbone took it from me back in the French Revolution after I swiped it from Holyrood. I've been following him halfway through this country trying to get it back. It's got to either be here in his tent or on him. But you're going to have to trust me if we're going to find it."

"Trust you?" Adelaide scoffed. "Says the girl who shot me back in Paris."

"I shot at you," Pauline spit back. "I was never actually going to hit you, I just wanted to stop you from bringing the earrings back and starting the blaze you unwittingly ignited when you did. Now are you going to get off me and help me find it or not?"

Adelaide removed her dagger and rolled off Pauline. Her mind was spinning as she worked her way to her feet. She held a hand down to Pauline, who clasped it and pulled herself up beside Adelaide.

As the intensity of her anger subsided, a dull ache settled in her head. She recalled what Father Jude had said about tuning out the noise of other stories and seeking out the one that calls loudest to her. Maybe she could do that with the journal. She closed her eyes, blocking out the sound of war that raged outside and turning her thoughts to her mother. As she did, the noise in her head seemed to quiet until a single voice called out to her like a whisper. She opened her eyes and approached the desk. Running her eyes and hands along the polished wood, Adelaide let the whispers in her head guide her.

"I already checked the desk." Pauline continued digging through the trunk.

Adelaide didn't respond, finding herself focused on the intricate carvings along the rim. She wasn't sure what drew her toward them until her eyes detected a flaw in the pattern. The carvings were a series of four-leaf clovers but hidden among them on the right-hand side was a clover carved with only three leaves. She brushed her thumb across it, fidgeting with the carving until it turned to match the direction of the others. As it clicked into place, a small panel on the top popped open. Nestled inside was a red-leathered book.

Adelaide reached for the journal in the same moment Pauline's fingers also curled around it. Their skin brushed, igniting a *trace* in the air between them. Unlike her previous *traces* which unraveled in real time, this one moved at an increased speed, as if someone had taken a remote and set it to fast forward. Images slipped from one to the next, most blurred together and indistinguishable from each other, but others were clear enough to make out bits and pieces. They all seemed to be of the same girl, her flame-red hair present in every scene that sped by through the years of her life, but only a few were clear enough for Adelaide to discern.

The girl in a wedding dress as she walked through a French town to the church.

Lying beside a boy in a boat as they watched the painted clouds overhead.

Dressed in black as she rested a hand against a marble casket.

And finally, a woman resting her head on an executioner's block.

A shot split the air and shook Adelaide out of the *trace*, but not before she'd watched an axe sever the woman's head from her body and spill crimson blood across the stone floor. Nausea rolled in her stomach as she locked eyes with Pauline over the journal still clenched between them. Though neither of them spoke, Pauline's face told Adelaide everything she needed to know. Pauline had seen it too.

"What do we have here?" a man's voice said.

Adelaide whipped her head to the front of the tent where a man now stood, blocking the entrance. He wore a Union officer's jacket and had dark hair that covered his head, upper lip, and cheeks in a thick mass.

"Rathbone." Pauline slipped the journal behind her back.

A sly smile crawled up his lips as he unsheathed his saber. "Hand over the book, Pauline. Or are you going by something else now? Keeping track of your aliases has become quite a chore in and of itself, let alone chasing you through every period on this god-forsaken timeline."

Quicker than Adelaide could react, Pauline stole her dagger, sliced an opening in the canvas and shoved the journal into Adelaide's hands. "Run!" she said as she pushed Adelaide through the gash.

Adelaide stumbled. She didn't want to leave Pauline behind. If she died, everything the girl knew vanished with her. But without a weapon, Adelaide didn't have any other choice but to force her legs to carry her away from the tent. She didn't understand. Rathbone might have been a lesser-known name from American history, but he was a Union general, not a Confederate spy. At least that's what she had learned about him in her history books. Were they wrong, or was this version of the man the real one all along? And what did he want with her mother's journal?

Metal clanged behind her, and a man's scream split the air as Adelaide searched for the horses. Having come undone in the fight with Pauline, her hair tumbled loose over her shoulders as she ran. She crossed the camp in the direction of the road and was almost back to Grant's tent when something solid knocked into her side. She landed hard on the ground and dropped the journal. She reached toward it, but a hand tangled in her hair and yanked her away with a ferocity that rattled her bones. A cry of pain escaped her lips as Rathbone threw her back to the ground and picked up the journal.

He advanced, forcing Adelaide to scuttle backward to avoid being sliced by his saber. Her back hit the solid wood of a cart, trapping her. Blood darkened his coat at the shoulder from a fresh wound. His sword grazed her collar bone, teasingly slicing a hole in the fabric of her blouse. He swung the blade lower, poising it directly over her chest. Her breath fell heavily as she waited for Rathbone to run her through.

A fist collided with his face. The impact knocked him to the side and sent his saber flying several feet before clanging to the ground. Teo slipped between her and Rathbone. He swung his arm in a wide arc, but this time Rathbone was ready for him. He dodged Teo's punch and seized his wrist, using his forward momentum to wrench him to the side. Teo thudded to the ground and attempted to rise, but Rathbone landed a kick to his stomach. Teo's wheezed, the air knocked out of his lungs.

Adelaide scrambled to her feet and retrieved the journal from where Rathbone had dropped it. A sickening crunch resounded behind her, and she turned to see Rathbone hit the ground beside Teo. His foot jutted to the side at an awkward angle. Teo rose to his feet and Rathbone tried to do the same, but the injury to his ankle gave way and he landed in a heap once more.

Anger flared in Teo's eyes as he cut his gaze to her. He gripped Adelaide's hand and pulled her away through the camp. This time she let him.

Rathbone's voice filtered to her hears as he shouted at a soldier behind her. "Ashburn, fetch me a horse and pistol. Now!"

"Pauline!" Adelaide yelled as they ran, trying to make herself heard over the clamor of gun fire and screams.

They broke through the edge of camp. Adelaide could finally see Kolt and the horses only a few yards off. He sat on Blackjack and held the reins of Apollo as he tried to settle the stallions, who were skittish at the clamor of war. They stomped their hooves on the dirt road and kicked up a cloud of dust around them.

Pauline materialized beside her. A fresh bruise colored the girl's temple and blood clotted on a swollen split down her lip. "Do you have it?"

Adelaide slowed as they neared the horses and showed Pauline the journal.

"Woah," Kolt said to the horses as he turned around. "Hurry. We don't have much time before—his eyes landed on Pauline. "Sienna?"

"Kolt," Pauline paled. "You remembered me. How—"

A bullet embedded itself in the ground at Blackjack's feet. The horse, Kolt in its saddle, reared. Behind Pauline, Rathbone galloped on a white steed. He gripped a steaming pistol in his hand.

Adelaide scrambled onto Apollo and helped Teo up behind her.

Pauline was still rooted in place. Kolt held out a hand to her expectantly, but she stayed put. "I can't..." Her gaze flicked between Kolt, the journal and Rathbone advancing.

Kolt's eyes widened, and Adelaide could see the fear spread through him. "Get on the damn horse, Sienna. I am not losing you again."

A second shot hit near Pauline's feet. It must have been enough to convince her because she sprang for Kolt. He grabbed her hand and swung her up behind him.

They raced back toward Richmond, only stopping to switch out horses at the closest paddock. Adelaide felt bad about stealing someone else's horses and leaving Elizabeth's behind, but there was no way they would outrun Rathbone and the other men he rallied behind him with the two they had. The stop alone set them back, and with each moment that passed the men edged closer.

Finally, they flew into the clearing and Adelaide jumped off the horse before she'd even pulled it to a complete stop. The others quickly dismounted. Kolt ran to the hidden time machine and turned it visible. The door whorled open as the pound of hoofbeats and shouts of men drew closer.

"Where do you think you're going?" Teo grabbed Pauline's arm as she tried to run away.

She glared at him. "Hiding before Rathbone gets here. I told you, I can't go with you."

"But—" Kolt started.

"Fine," Adelaide said.

"What?" Teo said as all three of them looked at her.

"Fine," Adelaide repeated. "If she doesn't want to come, we can't force her and we don't have time to argue about it."

Teo released Pauline as Kolt protested. She turned to head deeper into the woods as Adelaide slid a small vial from a pocket in her dress and poured the contents on her sleeve. Before Pauline could get far, Adelaide grabbed her from behind and clamped a sleeve covered hand over the girl's mouth. She held tightly as Pauline struggled, waiting until her movements had finally slowed to release her. Adelaide laid her gently on the ground and turned back to the boys, shock evident on their faces.

"Load her in and let's go."

30

TRUTH IN LIES

———

Adelaide opened her eyes to the flicker of colored lights in the dim of the time machine. White noise rang in her ears as she sat up and fumbled for the seatbelt strapping her in. Teo and Kolt, their clumsy movements a mix of time travel and adrenaline, did the same. Raising to her feet on shaky legs, Adelaide stood and reached for the button that opened the door.

"Don't," a soft voice croaked.

Adelaide dropped her hand and looked to the floor where Pauline was stirring. Her eyes blinked slowly as she fought against the aftereffects of the chloroform. Adelaide ignored her and opened the door.

Bright light from the apparatus floor flooded in. She held a hand to her face, shielding her eyes as Kolt helped Pauline to her feet and slung her arm across his neck to support her. Adelaide couldn't believe it. She'd actually found Pauline, and in turn, Kolt had found Sienna. She still wasn't sure what made the girls one and the same or how all the pieces fit together, but soon Pauline would be recovered and Adelaide would get her answers.

She smiled at the thought of knowing and finally being able to feel like she could breathe again, but the moment didn't last long. As her feet hit the cement floor, Adelaide realized they were not the only ones in the room.

Matriarch stood several yards from the catwalk stairs. Despite the still-late hour of the night, she was dressed in the dark-grey tones of a starched pantsuit. Her silver hair hung down her back in a pleat. She curled her long fingers together and rested her twined hands in front of her.

Xander was nowhere in sight, but Charlie remained. The hands of an armed guard gripped each of her shoulders and kept her rooted in place, standing a few feet away from the controls. Her eyes widened with fear and apology as they looked at Adelaide. "Ad, I'm sorry." Charlie started. "She found out—"

A slap across her face by the guard silenced Charlie. She slowly drew her head back and bit her lip against tears that threatened to fall as she raised a hand to her reddening cheek.

"Grandmother!" Kolt strained against the weight of Pauline.

Matriarch's slate eyes darkened. "Refuse to cooperate and a bruised cheek will be the least of Ms. Smith's worries."

She nodded to Charlie's guard who removed his gun and pressed the muzzle into her side. Charlie's breath hitched as the cool metal settled between her ribs and a tear slipped down her cheek. Charlie's wild eyes met hers, and Adelaide's stomach clenched as fear spread like a chill down her spine.

"Let's start with your gun, Mr. Capone." Matriarch motioned at Teo. "Remove it, slowly, and hand it to Hatfield."

Teo's jaw clenched, but after a glance at Charlie, he complied and relinquished his weapon to the nearest guard. "Anything else you'd like?"

"Me," Pauline said, her voice still weak, but stronger than before. "She wants me."

"What?" Kolt's jade eyes flicked between Matriarch and Pauline in confusion.

"Interesting." A knowing smile spread across Matriarch's face. "You remember her, but you don't remember what happened. Turns out some things you just can't erase—love, hate," she paused, "and power." Turning to Adelaide, she added. "I suppose I should thank you, my dear. We could have never gotten Sienna back or found your mother's journal without you."

Adelaide reeled. "What?"

Matriarch laughed, the sound cold and hollow in the large room. "Did you honestly think you could steal the time machine without anyone knowing. Or that it would be as easy as blacking out a few cameras and sneaking in between the guards' shifts?"

Adelaide's mind was slowly arranging some of the missing pieces into a picture that made sense. "You wanted us to take it. Civil War Richmond was never about Elizabeth. It was about finding Sienna and the journal."

And in her desperation for answers, Adelaide had just hand delivered both to Matriarch on a silver platter.

"Right you are, my dear," Matriarch crossed the room to Adelaide. "But it was also about much more than that."

Teo stiffened beside her as Matriarch raised a hand to Adelaide's face and grazed her knuckles across her cheek. Sweat beaded on Adelaide's palms, but she held the woman's gaze refusing to let her see her flinch.

"You see." Matriarch grasped Adelaide's chin and forced her head up to meet her own. Her fingers felt like ice and drew blood as the stone on her ring pierced Adelaide's skin. "You and Sienna here share a particular gift and I, for one, would like to know what it is and why."

Adelaide wrenched her chin from Matriarch's grasp and cut her gaze back to the woman's. Adelaide weighed her words carefully, not wanting to give Matriarch any information she didn't already have. "If you're talking about bringing the items back, what makes you think we understand it?"

"I'm not under the impression that either of you do." Matriarch's eyes slid to the journal in Adelaide's hand. "But I think your mother did."

Adelaide gripped the journal tighter to her side.

Noticing the motion, Matriarch tilted her head at Adelaide with curiosity. "Don't you want to know what it says?"

Adelaide remained silent. Of course she did, but whatever Matriarch's intentions were for wanting to know, she didn't trust they were good.

Matriarch nodded as if she could sense Adelaide's thoughts and stepped around her. She let out a shaky breath. As she turned to follow Matriarch with her gaze, her eyes connected with Teo's.

"What about you?" Matriarch approached Pauline. "Aren't you the least bit curious or are you as stubborn as your sister?"

Adelaide stilled as Matriarch's words washed over her. "Sister?"

The woman looked back to her. "You didn't know? Well neither did I until your blood taken by the door at the gala flagged as a sibling match to Sienna's from her initiation."

Adelaide swung her eyes to Pauline, expecting the girl to be equally shocked, but a whole other emotion entirely splayed across her face. Adelaide swallowed. "You knew."

Pauline stiffened, her voice still slow from the chloroform. "Yeah, Anna told me the night of the fire."

Silence weighed in the room as Adelaide tried to process all the new information, but it ricocheted around her head, making her feel like she had whiplash. She didn't understand. How could she have a sister she didn't know about. It didn't make sense, and yet, it also did. Though she couldn't explain how, Pauline had known who she was in Paris and what she could do. And while their abilities, themselves, were still a mystery, it could explain why they shared them.

Matriarch, her voice sharp like a double-edged sword, broke the silence. "Why don't we talk about the fire, huh? Because I, for one, would like to know what happened and why you were the only one to walk out of the flames."

Adelaide had to remind herself to breathe while waiting for Pauline's answer, but the girl remained silent.

Matriarch raised an eyebrow. "Very well." She motioned once again to Charlie's guard. "Make it quick, Adams. I'd hate to ruin the floor."

Charlie struggled against Adams as he shoved his gun farther into her side. "No, please!"

"Anna!" Pauline shouted.

Matriarch held a hand up, stopping Adams. "What?"

Pauline winced, knowing it was too late to take her words back. Adelaide hoped she had heard the girl's answer wrong, but as Pauline repeated it, she met Adelaide's gaze with sympathy in her heavy eyes. "Anna started the fire."

Adelaide's knees buckled as blood pounded in her ears. She would have fallen to the ground had Teo not caught her. Hot tears streamed down her face. "Why?"

"Because the Red Rose Society is trying to change history and they think I," Pauline paused, realizing the error in her words, "we, are the key to doing it. Anna set the fire to help me escape, burn what she'd discovered, and keep them from learning about you."

Matriarch closed the gap between her and Pauline. She grabbed the girl's arm and dug her nails into her pale flesh. "My daughter died in that fire." She leaned in. Her eyes held a glint sharp enough to sever bone. "So, if I were you, I would tell me everything Anna told you or things will start to get very unpleasant."

Kolt did what he could to shield Pauline from his grand-mother, but it wasn't much with her weight against him. Her head lolled as her eyes fought to focus on Matriarch.

All at once, Pauline lunged. Silver flashed in her hand, and Adelaide had just enough time to register that it was her own dagger before it sliced a red line across Matriarch's cheek. The older woman recoiled, and the guards that had been stand-ing around the room rushed in toward them at its center. Adelaide snapped to her feet and stood numb in the crowd, unable to get herself to move. Teo threw a punch and pushed the guards back best he could as Kolt ran to the time machine. He opened the door before climbing inside and starting the gears. It whirred to life, sending a violent gust across the apparatus floor.

Charlie elbowed her guard in the gut and launched herself at the controls. Her fingers flew across the buttons, and the turning gears picked up speed as she met Adelaide's eyes and yelled, "Go!"

A shot cracked with the wind, and Adelaide watched as Charlie fell against the control panel. A steady trail of blood ran slick across the buttons.

"Charlie!" She started to run toward her friend, but Teo caught her in his arms. She clawed against him as more tears streamed down her face, blurring her vision. He threw her back in the direction of the time machine. His face fought emotion as he repeated Charlie's words. "Go!"

A sob escaped her lips, and she turned on her heel. She sprinted up the steps and into the machine. Her arms fumbled with the belt as she strapped herself in and yelled to Kolt in a shaky voice, "Is it ready?"

"Almost," he yelled back as he shoved his com set on his head and paled, realizing no one would be on the other end.

Adelaide flinched as bullets ricocheted off the time machine and threw her gaze out the door. Teo sucker punched a guard in the stomach. He ran toward the time machine and threw Pauline's arm around his shoulder as he passed her, helping her along. Bullets peppered the air again. Teo grunted and staggered as a steady spread of blood soaked through his shirt near his stomach.

"You fools," Matriarch bellowed. "I need them alive."

Taking on Teo's weight, Pauline threw his arm around her shoulder and crossed the last few paces to the time machine. Adelaide helped her deposit Teo on the floor. She reached for the girl to pull her the rest of the way in but her hand clasped air as Pauline was pulled backward through the door. Adelaide had just enough time to register a flowered necklace, much like her own, slip out from under Pauline's shirt before Charlie's hand slapped the button on the control panel, and the door closed. A buzzing sound began to build in her head, but Adelaide could do little more than grip her mother's journal tightly in her arms and watch a loose page slip to the floor as darkness claimed her.

To unravel the mysteries that continue to plague Adelaide, look for book three in the *Crimson Time* series.

ACKNOWLEDGMENTS

Fractured Past would not exist were it not for all of the incredible people who have walked this journey with me.

I'd like to thank the following:

My family—for the endless love and encouragement.

Reilly Vore—for being the first to hear any of my stories and dreaming alongside me.

Abbey Frisco—for sharing a love of story and cheering me on from wherever you are.

Alyssa Dixon—for constant support and laughter when I need it.

Dwight Brautigam, Tim Smith, and Jeffrey Webb—for seeing the potential in the quiet girl at the back of the class and helping me see it myself.

Huntington University History Department—for cultivating my love of the past and encouraging me to make my mark.

Molly Rose—for challenging me in my writing and helping me build the roots of this story.

Eric Koester—for giving me the tools to bring this series to life.

Brian Bies—for helping me craft a beautiful book.

Haley Newlin—for being the genesis of this incredible journey and encouraging me every step of the way.

Alexander Pyles and Carol McKibben—for using your love of words to walk with me in various stages throughout the development of this series.

Lastly, I would like to thank everyone who supported me during my pre-sale by pre-ordering *Fractured Past*, donating to the campaign, or spreading the word. Thank you for being the first ones to be excited about my story.

Reilly Vore
Eric Koester
Abigail Pitsilides
Amber VanderBent
Ali VanderBent
Jaden VanderBent
Sue Coveney
Kelsie & Jacob Vore
Emmy Williams

Sydney Mueller
Kelsey Hunsberger
Kyra Ann Dawkins
Molly Burton
Hanna & Ethan Kamp
Marissa Miller
Mark & Ruth VanderBent
Kim DeBraal
Jill Slager

Hannah Johnson
Arlene DeYoung
Joyce Torrence
Gina Randol
Norris Friesen
Kim Brown
Melissa Kadich
Jordan Moore
Jessika Rucker
Grace Hasson
Haley Newlin
Sara Keith
Carol Knott
Tom & Lori Kamp
Tiffany Paris
Tessa Buiter
Kathy Petrarca
Beth Huegel
Patti Swets
Abbey Frisco
Nathan Fosnough
Alyssa Dixon
Dave VanderBent
Luz Cabrales
Noah Venhuizen
Hannah Britton
Lilian Sue
Samantha Iwinski
Michaela Perry
Faith Duncan
Julie Van Drunen
Karyssa Bolen

Reggie Greenwood
Mark Dold
Jen Rockey
Hanna Newlin
Sherilyn Emberton
Gary & Barb VanderBent
Amy Dong
Brittany Guiliani
Chris Chlebek
Cindy Smith
Becky Newhuis
Steve & Cheryl Vore
Gina Gill
Ruth Maynard
Kaitlin Gil
Martha Smith
Daren DeBoer
Tim & April VanderBent
Clayton & Jackie Denton
Juliet & Benjamin Kratz
Abigail Field
Tuesday Gallagher
Alec & Angelica Boyd-Devine
Kimberly Paris
Alexandra Tinsley
Brandon Posivak
Sharon Anderson
Teresa Rust
Brianna Guiliani
Shelby Kochel
Jennifer Welsh
Anonymous Donor

APPENDIX

—

CHAPTER 2

"Battle of Langside." Historic Environment Scotland. http://portal. historicenvironment.scot.designation/BTL35.

Fraser, Antonia. *Mary Queen of Scots*. New York: Dell Publishing, 1969.

CHAPTER 9

Fraser, Antonia. *Mary Queen of Scots*. New York: Dell Publishing, 1969.

CHAPTER 11

Abbott, Karen. *Liar, Temptress, Soldier, Spy*. New York: Harper Collins, 2014.

"Nurses for the Army." *Richmond Dispatch*, June 10, 1861. https:// mail.civilwarrichmond.com/written-accounts/newspapers/ richmond-dispatch/342-1861-06-10-richmond-dispatch-women-who-want-to-be-nurses-should-apply-to-mrs-a-f-hopkins.

CHAPTER 12

Abbott, Karen. *Liar, Temptress, Soldier, Spy.* New York: Harper Collins, 2014.

CHAPTER 19

Rosenberg, Jennifer. "The Story of Bonnie and Clyde." ThoughtCo. August 5, 2019. https://www.thoughtco.com/bonnie-parker-poem-bonnie-and-clyde-1779293.

CHAPTER 20

Fraser, Antonia. *Mary Queen of Scots.* New York: Dell Publishing, 1969.

CHAPTER 23

Abbott, Karen. *Liar, Temptress, Soldier, Spy.* New York: Harper Collins, 2014.

Rosenberg, Jennifer. "The Story of Bonnie and Clyde." ThoughtCo. August 5, 2019. https://www.thoughtco.com/bonnie-parker-poem-bonnie-and-clyde-1779293.

CHAPTER 24

Abbott, Karen. *Liar, Temptress, Soldier, Spy.* New York: Harper Collins, 2014.

CHAPTER 25

Abbott, Karen. *Liar, Temptress, Soldier, Spy.* New York: Harper Collins, 2014.

CHAPTER 27

Abbott, Karen. *Liar, Temptress, Soldier, Spy.* New York: Harper Collins, 2014.

CHAPTER 28

Abbott, Karen. *Liar, Temptress, Soldier, Spy.* New York: Harper Collins, 2014.

CHAPTER 29

Abbott, Karen. *Liar, Temptress, Soldier, Spy.* New York: Harper Collins, 2014.

ABOUT THE AUTHOR

———

Emily VanderBent is a writer and historian. A natural-born storyteller, she desires to relay and celebrate the stories of women in history. Through the *Crimson Time* series, Emily uses elements of history to creatively engage readers with the past. She hopes her writing will encourage young women to fearlessly pursue their passions and own the narrative of their individual story.

With a degree in history, Emily uses her talent for writing, research, and design to create blog posts, online content, and design for Girl Museum. She also helps walk authors through the publishing process as an Author Coach for New Degree Press. While living in the real world, Emily dreams of days long past and stories yet to be told.

For up-to-date information on the *Crimson Time* series and Emily's other publications, as well as access to writing resources and events, visit Emily's website and blog:

www.emilyvanderbent.org

You can also connect with Emily on the following social media platforms:

Instagram: emilyvanderbent_author
Pinterest, Goodreads, LinkedIn: Emily VanderBent
Facebook: Emily VanderBent: Author
Twitter: emvan6